"Will you spend time with your father while you're here?"

"No!" John's sharp retort crushed Grace's question almost before she finished asking it. "Besides, you said yourself that I'm healing faster than you expected."

Grace hadn't exactly said that, but she knew what the implication was: to flee as soon as he could.

"I don't know what happened between you and your father," she began tentatively, "but I know him and he's a good man."

"I know you think you know my father, Grace," he said. "But you don't."

"May I ask what he did that was so wrong?"

The pause before John answered seemed endless.

"He loved alcohol more than anything or anyone, and if you think that doesn't leave scars, well... All I can say is that you're wrong."

The secret Grace kept screamed so loudly inside her head she feared for a moment that she might blurt something out.

Because if he knew the role that alcohol had played in her own life, he wouldn't want her anywhere near him.

Donna Gartshore loves reading and writing. She also writes short stories, poetry and devotionals. She often veers off to the book section in the grocery store when she should be buying food. Besides talking about books and writing, Donna loves spending time with her daughter, Sunday family suppers and engaging online with the writing community.

Books by Donna Gartshore

Love Inspired

Instant Family
Instant Father
Finding Her Voice
Finding Their Christmas Home
A Secret Between Them

Visit the Author Profile page at LoveInspired.com.

A Secret Between Them

DONNA GARTSHORE

LOVE INSPIRED

INSPIRATIONAL ROMANCE

LOVE INSPIRED®
INSPIRATIONAL ROMANCE

Recycling programs
for this product may
not exist in your area.

ISBN-13: 978-1-335-59879-0

A Secret Between Them

Love Inspired
22 Adelaide St. West, 41st Floor
Toronto, Ontario M5H 4E3, Canada
www.LoveInspired.com

Printed in U.S.A.

For nothing is secret, that shall not be made manifest; neither any thing hid, that shall not be known and come abroad.
—*Luke* 8:17

As always:

For God with gratitude for the creative spirit
You have given me.

My family with love for all your support.

For my daughter, Sara—watching you live your
best life makes me strive to live mine.

Also, to Gordon. Your talent and profound gift for
helping people dig deep and find the best they
have to offer is appreciated more than I can say.

Chapter One

John Bishop had traveled extensively and done everything from balance on the edge of a cliff to swim with sharks, all to capture the perfect photo. So it was more than a little humiliating to be brought down by a child's skipping rope.

He didn't know that kids still jumped rope, or maybe they just did things like that in places like Living Skies, Saskatchewan, a place with the kind of homespun charm that could make you believe that life was all about jumping rope, singing songs in church and baking apple pies.

Of course, John knew from experience that not everything in Living Skies was picture-perfect.

The pain that ripped through him when he tried to shift to a more comfortable position wasn't just from his badly sprained ankle.

John suppressed a moan, but the receptionist at the front counter of the Elmview Physical Therapy Clinic still looked up with a sympathetic smile.

"The physical therapist is almost finished with her current client," she said encouragingly. "She'll be with you soon."

John nodded, stoic again.

"I don't think I've seen you here before," the receptionist continued, clearly now in the mood for friendly chitchat, which John was definitely *not* in the mood for. She tapped her name tag with a long manicured fingernail. "I'm Renee."

She appeared to be in her early twenties and had short red hair so bright that it couldn't be natural, two piercings in each ear and brown eyes staring out through oversize glasses. "You going to be here long or just passing through?"

If he had his way, he would have never set foot in Living Skies again. He'd only spent a few years here, part of the stream of events that took his father and him from one place to another with the ever-dwindling hope that his father would finally find that one place, that one job, that one reason to sober up. John, who'd been in his last few years of high school at the time, had longed for the kind of home he used to have before his mother left when John was eight, taking his little brother with her.

There were things that could hurt more than a sprained ankle or any broken bone or disease. There was a pain so raw and excruciating that the only way to survive it was to shove it way deep down and let scar tissue grow over it.

"I'm just here for a short time." He didn't want to be rude, but he didn't want to encourage conversation or add that this ankle business was going to make his stay longer than he'd hoped it would be.

Apparently, it didn't take much to encourage her, because she settled her elbows comfortably on the counter, intertwined her fingers and flexed them a bit, clearly gearing up for a good long chat.

"Who are you visiting?" she asked. "Do you have family here? I probably know them."

John swallowed. It was such a simple question for most, but to him, it was impossible to answer.

Yes, my father lives here. No, we're not family.

"I'm here to check things out at *The Chronicle*," he said, naming the town's newspaper.

It was true that the newspaper needed a new editor, but the chances of him taking the job were slim to none. He couldn't wait to get out of this place. But Stew Wagner, the retired editor of the paper, the man who had given a scared, bitter young man the chance to find his passion and prove himself, had asked him to at least come and check things out.

"Oh, that's cool," Renee said. "But now

you've gone and injured yourself. How'd you manage that?" John was saved from the embarrassment of that explanation when an office door opened and a woman who looked to be a few years younger than his thirty-five—attractive in an easy, no-fuss kind of way—stepped out. She had an athletic build, intelligent green eyes and dark blond hair pulled off her face into a ponytail. She cupped her hand under the elbow of the elderly man with her and spoke to him with a gentle expression.

After she and the client reached the door and said their goodbyes, she turned toward the almost empty waiting room, a gentle expression giving way to one of expectation. "Who's next?"

"This guy." Renee pointed at John. It didn't seem that formalities were a big thing here.

Renee swiveled her chair, picked up a file and extended it to the PT. "Doctor sent this over."

The PT took it and flipped it open briefly. "I'm Grace Severight. Come on, I'll help you into my office."

John wanted to protest and say that he could manage a few steps by himself, but he was smart enough to know when to accept help. The crutches he'd been using weren't cutting it.

He had heard once that medical professionals were discouraged from wearing strong scents because of the emotional impact it could have on patients. When Grace Severight came close to him, he could smell nothing but clean skin and the lingering trace of light soap, but his heart still slammed in his chest.

Somehow, it was a scent more powerful and personal than if she'd been doused in expensive perfume.

Grace was all professional efficiency, maneuvering herself into the best position to support him. He was glad that the distance to her office was short because of his injured foot and the strange reaction he was having to her closeness.

Her office was reasonably sized and displayed her educational credentials and a couple of pictures of scenic views. He glanced at the photos with a critical eye as he sat on the edge of the examination table. She didn't appear to be much of one for frippery.

She studied his file for a moment in silence and then glanced up. "So, this happened when you tripped over a skipping rope?" To her credit, she didn't make the cause of his injury sound nearly as ridiculous as she could have.

A simple nod would be enough of a response, but something in her calm, waiting expression made him want to volunteer more information. "It happened a few days ago. I was checking a message on my phone and not paying attention. I don't have a doctor here so I saw one at a walk-in clinic. They took X-rays and then referred me to you."

Grace nodded. "Yes, phones can be bad that way. They can really distract a person."

Distract was one word—*dismay* and *anger* were others.

The message that had distracted him had been yet another from his father, who swore he was sober now and wanted to make amends. The only reason he had John's number in the first place was that, despite everything, John couldn't quite bring himself to be unreachable in the case of an emergency. But that didn't include sitting down and making nice like the man hadn't inflicted years and a world of hurt upon him.

Not a chance.

"Is everything okay?" the PT asked.

John suspected she might be asking about more than his ankle. He had better reel in his emotions and fast.

"Yes, all good. So what's the fastest way to heal this thing?"

His list of objectives was short and to the point: heal the ankle, make a cursory check on the status of the newspaper, give some reason why he couldn't accept the job as editor and get on the road again.

He always wanted—needed—to be the one who left first.

"How about we start by having a look at it?" Grace said in an unruffled way.

She wheeled her chair over to the examination table where he sat.

"Let's see," she murmured as she rolled up his pant leg. It was late August, no longer quite warm enough for shorts, especially as the evenings tended to cool down considerably here.

Her touch was practiced and careful. Nevertheless, John flinched when her fingers explored the swelling around his ankle. He noticed that unlike the talons of the office receptionist, Grace's nails were clipped short and were clean and free of polish.

"That hurts." It wasn't a question. She stopped her probing, which he was more relieved about than he wanted to say, and wheeled back to the file on her desk to make a note.

Okay, so it hurt. He was still going to do whatever it took to get himself out of this town and on the road as fast as possible.

"Okay," Grace said efficiently. "I want you to try something for me. Try moving your ankle like you're writing out the letters of the alphabet."

"The alphabet?" John repeated.

"Yes, please. Try to move it in the shape of each of the letters."

The degrees on the wall, which John noted

she'd received with great distinction, told him that this woman was supposed to know what she was doing.

A. He gritted his teeth.

B. His nostrils pinched together in a sharp intake of breath.

C. Sweat broke out on his forehead.

"Okay, that's good for now," Grace said and jotted another note.

"I can keep going," John said, sure he would sound much more convincing as soon as he caught his breath.

"No, it will cause more damage if we push things," Grace said. "We'd better go at this more slowly."

Slowly was definitely *not* a word he wanted to hear.

"Look," he said, employing his best reasonable tone, "I'm a photojournalist. I travel for a living, and I need to get back to work."

"I get that," Grace said in an equally reasonable tone. "But if we don't go about this the right way, you might not be traveling at all for a very long time."

"I only tripped over a kid's skipping rope." He shook his head at the absurdity of it all.

"And you did some pretty good damage to some ligaments. Now, here's what I want you to try before I see you again tomorrow."

John forced himself to listen to her instructions on leg elevation, compresses and ice packs, all while his mind frantically sought escape routes.

"Are you getting this?" Grace asked. "Because we have to be partners in your healing, otherwise it's not going to work."

"Got it," John said, wondering how he could ask exactly how slow *more slowly* would be. "It's just that I have jobs lined up for some major magazines."

Grace snapped the folder shut, looking unimpressed. "I'll get Renee to write out the instructions for you, and I'm going to count on you to follow them."

John nodded, not feeling very encouraged by the visit.

"You're not planning to be a difficult patient, are you, Mr. Bishop?" Grace asked with humor, but there was also a challenge in her voice.

"Nope, I'm going to do whatever gets me out of here the fastest."

A note of puzzlement crossed the PT's face, but she quickly regained her professional demeanor and didn't ask any questions.

When they exited her office, there was a middle-aged woman in the waiting room with a small boy who looked to be about five years old.

"I hope we haven't come too early," the woman said.

"Not at all. Your timing is perfect," Grace said. "Thank you so much for picking Toby up at the daycare. Hi, sweetheart, how was your day?"

There was something so vulnerable and delicately hopeful, like a slowly unfolding rose, in Grace's expression when she spoke to the boy that John suddenly longed to have his camera in his hand to capture the moment.

That thought was chased away when the boy lifted his face to her.

John hadn't set eyes on his little brother, Simon, in decades, not since he was eight years old and Simon was five. Grace's son, or whoever he was to her, fit so readily into the picture of Simon that John carried in his heart, that it took his breath away.

Each day, as many times as she needed to, Grace Severight told herself, *Today, I will not have a drink.* On particularly trying days, it was sometimes, *I won't have a drink this hour,* or even, *I won't have a drink for the next five minutes.*

She had been sober for ten years, and she thanked the Lord for each and every one of those days, because she knew she wouldn't have been able to do it on her own strength.

She wasn't at all the stereotypical drunk that people pictured when they thought about alcoholics. At the weekly meetings she attended—far enough from Living Skies for her to keep her secret from most everyone she had grown up with—she had learned that there really was no such thing as a typical drunk. They could be businessmen and women, housewives, pastors, daycare workers, athletes, poets—all with nothing more in common than their battle with alcohol.

Granted, some alcoholics could pinpoint horrible triggers—abuse, neglect and devastating tragedies—in their lives. But many of them, like Grace, had simply slipped into the addiction as easily as turning onto a winding path without knowing that somewhere along the road, they were going to skid out of control.

Grace was the only child of parents whose main rule in life seemed to be to not make a fuss or cause unnecessary trouble for anyone. When she told them of her struggles with drinking and her efforts to quit, they had only asked that she not shame them or make it more their concern than it had to be.

It had become something that she couldn't share.

Of course, she'd had to be honest in her application to foster Toby Bower, who had been with her since last Christmas. She had just about gnawed her fingernails down to the nail beds waiting for the Department of Social Services' response. Toby had been removed from a home where his young mother battled depression and substance abuse. Luckily, Grace's years of sobriety, combined with faithful meeting attendance, as well as her professional designation as a physical therapist and good reputation in the community, had turned things in her favor.

Still, it was something Grace never wanted to take for granted.

Along with being a physical therapist, Grace also did volunteer work, leading a regular health and wellness program that people could attend.

Lately, she had the goal of expanding those programs to include a variety of new learning opportunities—anything from artistic and creative endeavors to Bible studies and learning how to polka. She was always on the lookout for instructors. She wanted to bring the best people in the community to help her send out the message that no one is alone and that everyone can live their best life.

Right now, though, that lofty goal had faded in comparison to the goal of getting Toby Bower to open up to her about his day.

Grace thought about how Toby had come into her life. Her best friend, Jenny Hart, was married to David Hart, who was a family counselor. David had made some visits to Toby's home, where he lived with his mother, Tiffany, and had come to the sad conclusion that Tiffany was currently incapable of caring for her son.

She understood that her role was to provide safety, support and sustenance for Toby. The hope was that his mother would put enough effort into her own recovery to make a suitable parent for him. She knew that the goal was always to have the child raised by their birth parent. But in the deepest part of her giving heart, Grace wondered what it would take to adopt Toby and be his mother forever.

Grace unlocked the door of her two-bedroom bungalow, chatting casually the whole time just like Toby's social worker, Blanche Collins, had recommended. Much as Toby needed and undoubtedly craved attention, he could be easily overwhelmed by too much of it.

"I hope you had a good day," Grace said. "I had a pretty busy day. On my lunch break, I picked up some books from the library I think you might like. We can look at those after supper and your bath if you want."

Grace's home was much like her office: clean, organized and efficient. She favored earth tones with some brightly hued throw pillows to add pops of color.

"Guess what's for supper?" She continued chatting to the still-taciturn Toby as she led him into her kitchen. The walls there were light green, and there was a small table in the center with a couple of stools. Prior to Toby, Grace had most often sat at the kitchen counter for a quick bite, but now she used the table.

She put her keys and purse down on the counter and looked down at Toby. Her heart lurched. He was still so pale, so unhappy.

Panic infused her like an unwanted drug. He'd been with her now for a while. What if she simply couldn't make a breakthrough with him and it was decided he was better off elsewhere?

"Don't you want to guess?" She forced cheerfulness into her voice. The last thing Toby needed was for her to wallow in her fear of failure. This was about his needs, not her fears.

"I'll give you a hint. It's your favorite."

"Mac and cheese?" Toby ventured in his surprisingly deep voice.

Happiness and relief washed away the stains of doubt, but she resisted the urge to hug him. It was that paradox again—the more starved someone was for physical touch, the more likely they were to reject it.

Instead of a hug, she held her fist out for him to bump with his and said, "You're right! How'd you get so smart?"

Toby's smile was shy as he cautiously bumped fists with her.

"Why don't you go wash your hands," Grace suggested. "Then you can help me."

She tried to engage Toby as much as she could with the things she did. She hoped it would encourage him to learn, and more importantly, she hoped it would build trust between them. She wanted him to feel that they were a team and to know she wasn't going anywhere.

Of course, she knew that he could be taken from her one day, but she had to believe that if that happened, it would be for a good reason, like his mother being well enough to care for him.

Toby returned from washing his hands, and Grace helped him onto a kitchen chair to stand beside her at the counter. She put lettuce in the spinner and slid it over to him.

"Like this." She showed him how to turn the handle.

When he was busy with the lettuce, she allowed herself to think about the things she needed to do once he was tucked in bed. Most of them involved organizing the upcoming activities at the center.

She also found herself thinking about John Bishop. He was going to be a challenge. She could tell that after just the first appointment.

There was nothing worse than a patient who was in a hurry, and she had a feeling that he was used to getting his own way.

There was something about him that said he was prepared to do the things he had to do to get the results that he wanted. Whether that would work for her or against her during his treatment remained to be seen.

Toby turned to give the salad spinner back to her, and his feet in socks skidded on the chair.

"Whoa there, bud." Grace put a steadying arm around him while she scolded herself for letting her mind wander. Toby needed and deserved better than that.

For a moment, he leaned into her, and she could feel his heart beat like the quick flutter of a sparrow's wing. Then he pulled away and carefully got down.

At the kitchen table, Grace encouraged him with some prompting to say the blessing she had taught him and then served them both some mac and cheese and salad.

The rest of the evening passed too quickly, as it always did. After a cursory kitchen cleanup, Grace ran Toby's bath and laid out his pajamas.

"Any stories from your day?" she tried again as she scrubbed the back of his thin neck.

He shook his head vigorously.

She suppressed a sigh. "Okay then." She lifted him out of the tub and helped him dry off.

"Go get your pajamas on and pick out one of the library books. I'll be in right away to read to you and tuck you in."

The book he chose was one with few words, but it had glorious colored photographs of nature.

Grace slowly turned the pages, and she and Toby both pointed at things they especially liked. Toby giggled at a picture of a frog with its throat bulged out, and the sound warmed her heart.

After bedtime prayers and a kiss on her own fingertip that she then lightly tapped on his nose, Grace took the book downstairs with her. There was something soothing about the pictures. It was a reminder that there was a Creator in charge of things who cared about Toby and about her.

With Toby tucked in bed, she had time to look over her notes on the possible activities and consider who could lead them. It wasn't easy attempting to coordinate such an undertaking, but it suited Grace's organizational skills. Concentrating on the work also helped keep self-doubts that could gallop like wild horses somewhat safely corralled.

She made herself a cup of chamomile tea and

settled into her favorite armchair. Its blue-flow-ered pattern was starting to fade, but the back of it hugged her spine just right.

John Bishop said he was a photographer. She should check out those magazines he mentioned he worked with.

No, she shook her head. He was her client. The only thing that should matter was his in-jury and her treatment plan.

She couldn't ignore that he was attractive in the way that didn't come from expensive clothes and grooming products. His mere size was more than a bit intimidating, and his brown hair could use a good trim. There was something both in-tense and vulnerable in his blue-green eyes that made her wonder what his story was.

But her job was to deal with his injured ankle. She really had no reason to be thinking of him now.

No reason at all.

She was almost relieved when the phone rang, even though she generally disliked it when it interrupted her evenings. She hurried to pick it up, not wanting the ringing to wake up Toby.

"Hello?"

"Hello, Grace?"

"Yes, speaking." She immediately recognized the clear but slightly nasal voice of Bethany

Hoover, the director of Child's Garden Daycare, and her throat suddenly went dry.

She swallowed.

"I'm so sorry to call you at home," Bethany continued, "but you weren't the one who picked Toby up today. We need to make a plan to get together to chat and see if we can work something out about Toby."

"Work something out?" Grace repeated, and the wild horses broke out of their corral.

There was a slight pause. "I'm so sorry to tell you that Toby just isn't doing well at the daycare," Bethany said. "And if we can't find a way to work together to improve things, I'm afraid we might not be able to keep him in our program."

After they ended the call, Grace sat holding her phone and considered the repercussions. If she couldn't find a safe place for Toby while she worked, Social Services might reconsider her fostering him, especially since she was already doing this alone.

No, she reminded herself, she wasn't alone. God was with her and she would have to trust He would provide her with an answer.

Chapter Two

As far as motels went, the Sunset Motel was far from the worst place John had ever stayed in. In fact, it was really quite appealing, with its calming palette of pastel colors and comfortable bed with crisp, clean sheets. It even had a decent view of a park that was frequented by people of all ages and some pets.

The place would be perfect if only he could stop feeling sorry for himself that he was staying in a motel and didn't have a friend or family member here that he could make himself at home with. But then again, that was his choice, so he didn't exactly know why his solitariness was hitting him so hard.

Self-pity wasn't his style, so maybe his constantly aching ankle was getting to him more than he wanted to admit. Or maybe it was that attractive physical therapist and her calm certainty that his healing would be slow.

Well, he would just have to show her different.

Grunting, he pushed himself off the bed to a standing position. The constant ache rapidly flared into a piercing pain, and he collapsed onto the bed again.

After taking a few deep breaths to recover, John grunted in resignation and carefully reached over to where he had tossed the list of instructions he'd been given at therapy.

He was going to see Grace Severight again tomorrow morning, and he had absolutely no doubt that she would ask him if he'd followed her instructions. He wanted to be able to tell her yes, so he figured he had to do something about that.

He was a lot of things, but he wasn't a liar. He couldn't stand lies…or secrets. Being the child of an abusive alcoholic meant he'd suffered from far too many of those, and he believed that even brutal honesty was better than the whitest of lies.

Of course, the best thing was to not ever get close enough to someone so their lies could hurt. Not getting close to anyone also meant he never had to make the choice about how much to share.

Preparing to be honest and open with his physical therapist didn't count since she was only a means to an end.

A means to an end that smelled like fresh air in the morning at a northern lake.

Okay, he definitely couldn't let his thoughts go in that direction. He needed to apply ice packs and use the compression bandage as per instructions so that he could heal as quickly as possible. That was a better reason than wanting to impress the pretty PT with how well he could follow orders.

An hour later, with his ankle experiencing some relief from the ice and wrapped in a compression bandage as recommended, snugly but not tightly, John prepared himself to venture out to Murphy's Restaurant for a bite to eat.

Another advantage of the Sunset Motel was its close proximity to Murphy's Restaurant.

The front desk clerk had enthusiastically recommended it, and John had simply nodded and thanked her. He hadn't bothered to mention that he was already familiar with its reputation for delicious homemade food. He'd mostly avoided the place because of too many curious eyes. Even if some of the gazes were kind and well-meaning, all he ever felt here in town was scrutiny.

Balancing on his crutches as he used his shoulder to push the restaurant's door open, John had to remind himself that he'd moved on from Living Skies years ago. He was a grown man with a successful career, and he was just passing through.

He had purposely opted for a late supper to avoid the dinner rush. Still, when the friendly hostess told him to sit wherever he wanted, he chose the most unobtrusive table he could find and studied his surroundings over the top of the menu. The decor was homey and low-key, making the food and not the surroundings the star of the show.

As John studied the menu, vacillating between a burger with mushroom sauce and provolone cheese or a more healthy choice of salmon steak, he found himself thinking about the little boy that had been dropped off at the clinic just as he was leaving.

Once again, his fingers arched and itched in that peculiar way they did when he wanted to be holding his camera. When you looked at someone or something long enough through a camera lens, they eventually revealed something about themselves. Most of the time without knowing it—the flutter of an eyelash, the quick downward turn of a mouth just before a smile went back into place for a picture.

John chose to put his trust in the photographs he took and what he could see through his camera's lens, certainly not in people.

Did he trust in God? Now, that was a confusing one. It was hard to ignore the evidence of a loving and intelligent Creator in all the wonders of nature he had seen. But it was equally hard to say he had personally experienced evidence of that love.

Most of the time, he simply refused to dwell on the question.

He wondered if the little boy was Grace's son. Somehow, he didn't think so. It was just a vibe he got. There was something almost shy in the way she had greeted him. Like she wanted to make a good impression but wasn't sure how.

He shook his head. He shouldn't be thinking about whether or not his PT had kids. It was none of his concern. But he still couldn't shake the impact of how much the little boy reminded him of Simon.

The closest thing he got to a prayer these days was the fervent wish he made every day that Simon had a happy life.

A pretty Indigenous young woman wearing a name tag that said Michelle on her red-and-black-plaid uniform appeared at his table holding a coffeepot.

"Sorry for keeping you waiting," she said. "We just had a big party arrive. Are you ready to order? Would you like coffee or something else to drink?"

"Just water is fine, thank you," John said. His eyes scanned the menu once more, and he chose the salmon.

"Great choice." Michelle nodded approvingly.

Now that his order was in, John wished he had thought to bring a book to read. With nothing to distract him, the buzz of conversation of the party that had just been seated drew his attention.

There were some Bibles sticking out of bags, and he could hear bits of conversation, so he guessed they had just come from a Bible study or evening service of some kind.

Michelle delivered his water with the promise that his food would be along soon. He thanked her and sipped the water slowly, absorbing bits of the conversation without much effort or interest.

"Well, I can tell you," a voice rose up more distinctly from the nondescript murmur of the conversation, "there isn't a day that goes by that I don't thank the Lord for bringing me to my senses before it was too late."

I know that voice.

Water clogged in John's throat, and he coughed. He covered his mouth and muffled the sound in his elbow, wanting desperately not to bring attention to himself.

It had been years since he'd heard his father's voice, other than on brief phone calls that John had quickly terminated, but he recognized it. He would know it anywhere.

His eyes frantically scanned the restaurant for Michelle, and he waved her over.

"Something the matter?" she asked, her warm brown eyes shining with concern.

"It, ah, my ankle's bugging me more than I expected," John said in a low voice. It was true enough. It was throbbing again. "I'm sorry for the trouble, but could someone just run the food over to the Sunset when it's ready? That's where I'm staying. I'll pay a delivery fee, whatever it is."

"I can run it over myself," Michelle said. "We're not going to charge you for a few steps. Are you sure you're going to be okay?"

John nodded, though his pounding heart said otherwise. He gave her his room number and thanked her again.

He wasn't going to add to the drama he was already creating by asking if there was a back exit, so there was nothing he could do but make his way to the door. He could only hope that the years his father hadn't seen him would provide sufficient disguise.

"John?"

No such luck. His eyes swung without his permission in the direction of that familiar voice, but then he looked away again. Gritting his teeth against the pain, he made his way out of the restaurant as quickly as he could.

Later, back in his room, when his stomach had calmed enough for him to try a few bites of food—it was delicious, and he wished he had more appreciation for it—John thought about the split-second glance he'd had of his father.

George was clean-shaven now. In fact, everything about him looked clean…renewed.

But John didn't trust it. Not one bit.

He was suddenly anxious for the morning to come. He wanted to see Grace Severight again. He wanted to know everything he needed to do to heal so he could be on the move again.

He wanted her calm efficiency to chase away the turmoil that was eating him up inside.

It was Wednesday morning, and Grace had an appointment to meet with Bethany Hoover at the daycare that afternoon. There was nothing she could do about the situation until then, so there was no point in chasing worst-case scenarios around in her head.

Or so she kept trying to tell herself.

After Bethany's phone call, she had gone into Toby's room and watched him sleep for a few minutes, being careful not to disturb him. It saddened her that even in sleep he appeared guarded. He lay with his little arms wrapped around his chest.

She prayed that he would grow to trust her

and, more importantly, that he would trust that he was worthy of a happy future. She also prayed that the meeting with the daycare would be a positive one.

But now it was time to focus on the task at hand. She opened her office door and saw that John Bishop was already in the waiting room. He was flipping through an old magazine while fielding a barrage of questions from Renee.

Grace made a mental note to speak to Renee about that. The girl was friendly and meant well, but not everyone was up for spilling their life story. Still, a part of her wanted to wait and see just what Renee could get out of him.

Instead she said, "Come on in. Need any help?"

"Nope, I've got it." John made his way to her office.

"Nice chatting with you!" Renee called after him, and it was hard to know if the hard-set line of his mouth was because of his ankle or the receptionist's curiosity.

Probably a little of both, Grace concluded.

"So, how did it go last night?" she asked John when they were in her office.

"I put ice on the area like you said, and I did some of the exercises you suggested. I also put a compression bandage on it."

Grace tried not to smile at this somewhat robotic recitation.

There was something different about John this morning. Of course, she didn't know him well, or at all really, but she sensed something was troubling him. Something more than a sore ankle, of that she was sure.

"Let's have a look."

She wasn't going to ask him if he'd slept well. Her concern was his ankle.

"I think the swelling has gone down a bit," she said. This time he didn't wince as much under her probing fingers, but she suspected he would be the type to resist showing it. "So, the ice helped?"

"I think so, yes," John said.

She raised her gaze to his, and her breath caught in her throat. She was unprepared for the spark of connection that lit through her, and she reactively pulled her chair back a bit.

His scent was something like wind and pine, and it followed her even though she had put some space between them. He cleared his throat and shifted, as if he too had experienced something he didn't quite understand.

Grace busied herself with flipping papers in his file. Clearly she was more stressed out over the meeting later today than she wanted to admit. That was the only explanation for her unsettling reaction to him.

"Okay, keep doing that—the ice, I mean," she said, her voice a bit icy itself. "If the swelling continues to go down as I hope, we'll add some other exercises to the routine."

When she was sure she could trust her face, she snapped the file shut.

"I guess that's it for now," she said. "Come back and see me on Friday. Do you have any questions?"

"Yes. Is there, ah, a Bible study group or something here on Tuesday nights?"

John looked almost as surprised to have asked the question as Grace was to have heard it.

"Yes, there is," Grace said. "I don't attend myself because I like to be home in the evenings after working all day, but I hear it's a good group. Is it something you're interested in while you're here?"

His adamant headshake reminded her briefly of Toby.

"Just curious," he said. "I went out to get something to eat last night, and I saw a group in the restaurant. I thought that's what it must be."

There was a slight but unmistakable note of bitterness in his voice. Was he angry at God for some reason, Grace wondered, or at someone else?

He used the heel of his hand to push his too-long hair out of his eyes.

Grace didn't know why the question and this gesture made him suddenly seem so vulnerable, but an urge to comfort him rose up within her.

"I promise we'll get this ankle fixed up as soon as we can." She felt very sure that it was more than his ankle bothering him, but that was the best she could offer.

Still, she couldn't resist embracing her inner Renee and asking, "So, you went out to get something to eat. You're not staying with anyone in town?"

"I'm staying at the Sunset Motel," John said. The rigidly set line of his mouth had returned.

Grace let a beat of silence pass. She sensed he wouldn't welcome further questions. "It's a nice place, I know the owners."

John grinned a little and said, "Doesn't everybody know everybody in a place like this?"

The smile softened his face. He still wasn't traditionally handsome, but there was no denying he had a definite charm.

His comment about everyone knowing everyone toyed with her, and she thought about the secret she kept from most people. Once you had a secret, it was easy to imagine that others did too.

The silence in the room seemed filled with questions and speculation. There was nothing else to do or talk about at this appointment, but John lingered, and Grace's skin prickled with an odd anticipation.

Then he took a deep breath and asked in a rushed way, "The little boy who got dropped off yesterday… He's your…"

"He's staying with me," Grace said cautiously, wondering why this man would be asking. "I'm a foster parent. Why do you ask?" Her voice sharpened to a point as she folded her arms across her chest.

The affection mingled with pain on his face caused her defenses to lower slightly, but her question remained.

"He reminds me of… He reminds me of someone I used to know," John said.

For an agonizing moment, the husky note in his voice made Grace wonder if he was about to cry. Once again, a fierce protectiveness surged through her.

This was ridiculous, she told herself. The man looked like he wrestled grizzly bears and won. But she still couldn't readily shake the instinct that he needed to be sheltered from further harm.

Not that she was the person to do so. She would help get his ankle back in proper working order, and he would be on his way.

As if echoing her thoughts about being on his

way, John eased himself off the table and balanced himself against it as he prepared to leave.

"I'd better get going. I have a meeting I need to get to."

"A meeting?" Grace couldn't help asking. "I thought you were just passing through."

"I am," John said, setting his face in a determined way. "I mean, I will be." He worked his strong jaw a little as if considering how much more to say. "I got my start taking pictures for *The Chronicle*," he said. "I got a call from Stew Wagner recently. He's heard things have gone downhill, and he asked me to check it out."

"You're *that* photographer?" Realization dawned on Grace. "My friend Jenny Hart does some freelance work for the paper, and she raves about your pictures."

John ducked his chin into his chest in an unexpectedly shy and utterly appealing way.

"Stew was good to give me a chance," he said. "I owe him."

"Stew's definitely one of the good ones," Grace agreed. "We miss him around here, but I take it he's happy in Victoria, close to his family?"

It was too easy to slip into a conversational mode with John Bishop, and she didn't know if she should guard against that or enjoy it.

In the meantime, however, she still had a few

minutes before her next client, and she enjoyed hearing John share anecdotes about his former boss, who was known as quite a character in his own right.

She noted that John was not only a great photographer but a good storyteller as well. As she watched him, Grace thought that something about his facial expressions and the way he used his hands reminded her of someone.

George Bishop.

"Are you by any chance related to George Bishop?" she asked brightly as they exited her office. "He sometimes leads a Bible study as part of the activities I arrange at the community center. The way you tell stories reminds me of him."

John's entire body went stiff, and a thunderous cloud darkened his eyes.

"He's my father."

Grace had never heard the title of *father* spoken with such anger, bitterness and regret.

The George Bishop she knew was a decent man. Surely there must be some mistake. How could his name provoke such a reaction from John? But before she could say anything more, John made his way past her and was gone.

Grace breathed slowly in and out, trying to recover her equilibrium. She sent up a prayer that John would find peace from whatever, or whoever, it was that caused his obvious emotional pain.

She also said a prayer for herself. Between unintentionally offending a new client—and a man that she couldn't help having a soft spot for—and dreading the daycare meeting later, she was going to need all the help she could get.

Chapter Three

John eased his SUV into a parking spot close to *The Chronicle*'s office on Center Street. In a town the size of Living Skies, he would have really preferred to walk everywhere. It seemed ridiculous to use his car for such a short drive. It was just another way that his ankle was more than a literal pain.

But that was the least of his worries. His stomach knotted in regret over the way he left Grace Severight's office. She didn't deserve his behavior and was probably wondering what in the world was wrong with him.

Sometimes he wondered that himself.

The thing was, he had really been enjoying their conversation. For a few minutes there, it was like being with a friend, or at least a potential one. The kind competency she radiated had done even more than he'd hoped to soothe him, which was why hearing his father's name come out of her mouth had been such an unpleasant shock.

She knew nothing of his father's true nature and nothing of their past, so John knew that the hot anger that had erupted in him wasn't reasonable, not in the least.

Over the years, he had learned ways to identify and avoid the triggers that threatened to push him off the bridge of distance and detachment that he had so carefully built. But every so often, something like this would blindside him.

He inwardly vowed that he would apologize to Grace when the newspaper meeting was over. He wasn't prepared to go into detail or explain anything, but he would certainly apologize.

Being a photojournalist, John dealt primarily in images, but as soon as he stepped into the office of *The Chronicle*, he understood beyond doubt what people meant when they talked about how the sense of smell could provoke intense and emotional memories.

As he breathed in the scents of pinewood and paper, along with the aroma of percolating coffee that he knew would pack a wallop, John was suddenly eighteen years old again. He'd been so scared that life had nothing to offer him, or vice versa. He'd been scared of life in general, and Stew Wagner had peered at him over the rims of his black horned-rimmed glasses and asked if he was willing to learn.

He honestly couldn't even remember what had made him go into the newspaper office in the first place, except that the only time he had believed he might have a little something to offer was when he took photographs. He used to submit them to the school yearbook, and they'd used every single one of them.

"You're John Bishop." A woman John recognized as the one who had dropped off the little boy Grace was fostering came forward with a welcoming smile and an extended hand.

"I'm Vivian Russell. You probably don't remember me but I remember you from when you lived here before. I'm the receptionist here." She glanced around the office. "Not sure we really need one right now, but Stew hired me, and he's too loyal to fire me. I guess it's a good thing I have a few other hats to wear around town."

She had short curly hair that was starting to go gray and a slight overbite that added a bit of youthful whimsy to her smile.

John acknowledged that her face was familiar and fought the urge to ask Vivian how well she knew Grace and what she could tell him about her. He guessed it must be pretty well, at least well enough for Grace to entrust her with day-care pickup.

"Would you like some coffee?" Vivian asked. "Though I have to warn you, it will knock your socks off."

"I remember," John said and smiled.

"Oh, of course." Vivian smiled in return. "You worked here before my time but I'm very familiar with your reputation." She gestured at his photos. "And you're doing so well!"

"Thank you," John said as gracefully as he could manage. He did appreciate praise as much as any other person, but on some level, he still struggled to believe he deserved it. Besides, taking photographs was how he made sense of the world and how he allowed himself to get close to situations that he might not normally be comfortable in. He used his camera both as a way to seek the truth and as a barrier to help keep his own emotions at bay. It didn't seem quite right to accept praise for something like that.

Still, he knew that people meant well, so he had learned to put on a smile and thank them.

"I think we all got conditioned to make coffee this way," Vivian said, pouring them each a cup. "My hubby won't even let me put a pot on at home anymore. He insists on making it himself. Can't say I'm too sorry about that." She winked.

"Anyway, let's get Stew up on the computer here, and we can start our meeting."

Approximately forty-five minutes later, John

rubbed the back of his neck to try to ease away the tension that came with knowing he was right. Stew wanted more from him than he was prepared to give.

"We lost a good editor when Stew retired," Vivian said, adding to John's unease as she rinsed out their coffee mugs after the meeting. "Sadly, he was replaced by someone who cared more about stirring the pot than good journalism. I'm just going to say that I think you'd be good for this place."

"I appreciate that," John said. "But I just don't see myself settling here."

"Ah, but these days you can do your work from almost anywhere. Isn't that true?"

John cleared his throat and shifted uncomfortably.

"Oh, I'm sorry," Vivian said. "Your ankle must be killing you. I'm sure it can't be easy to make any kind of decision while you're in pain."

John didn't bother telling her that his decision had already been made, and his ankle healing wasn't going to change any of that.

"I saw you at Grace Severight's office when I dropped Toby off," Vivian added with the ease of small-town sharing. "She's one of the best, and a lovely woman. You're in good hands."

The words made a red blush crawl up the back of John's neck like he was a schoolboy. Fortunately, Vivian had momentarily turned her back on him and didn't notice.

Then he thought of what she'd said. The little boy's name was Toby. It felt important to him to know that.

"So, you know Grace well, then?" He told himself that he was asking because it was better than continuing to discuss a job he had no intention of taking. Maybe he could put out feelers for a suitable replacement while he was here, but it certainly wasn't going to be him.

"I do." Vivian nodded. "She's a wonderful woman, as I said. She's a fine physical therapist and an even better person. So pretty too, don't you think?"

Now her gaze on John was a bit too intent for his liking.

"She's single too."

And that was his cue to excuse himself.

"My only concern is that she's as good a PT as you say," John said stiffly. The last thing he needed was Vivian or anyone else getting ideas. "Thank you for the coffee and everything. It was nice to see you again," he said politely.He didn't really remember much about Vivian but that was because he had lived in a cocoon of fear and secrets.

"You too," Vivian said. "We'd love it if you would consider being the editor here."

John wanted to say he would think about it to ease his exit, but that simply wasn't true.

Vivian's words about what a wonderful and attractive woman Grace was itched at him. John's throat was dry, and his breath grew a bit shallow at the thought of seeing her again to apologize. He was in his car. He could just keep on heading right out of town and drive until he found wherever his next destination was. There were qualified physical therapists all over the place.

But the little boy, Toby, and his resemblance to Simon tugged at him. Not to mention he couldn't live with himself if he didn't apologize for his earlier behavior.

Something about Grace also tugged at a part of him, the part that he kept closed off. He just wouldn't think about that. He had always believed that loving meant sharing everything about yourself, including your past, and he didn't think he was ever going to be ready to do that.

As John turned his vehicle in the direction of the physical therapy clinic, he saw his father stopping to plug money into a newspaper stand and take out a paper.

For a moment, his hands shook so badly on the steering wheel that he thought he might have to pull over.

Another memory took over, an unexpectedly positive one of his father reading the newspaper at the breakfast table, occasionally chuckling and making an observation out loud and taking the time to explain to John why one particular story or another was important.

It was one of the few times he felt safe around his father, though now he realized he'd forgotten that there was ever a time he felt that way.

So, his father still liked reading the newspaper. That didn't matter to him. It didn't matter at all.

Except he knew now that it was one more thing he wouldn't be able to stop thinking about. At least he could get his apology to Grace over with, and they would see where things went from there.

He hoped that she would accept, because despite his impulsive thoughts about leaving town, he really didn't want anyone but her to be his PT.

I will not have a drink tonight.

Grace had called her sponsor and taken time to pray, and she trusted that the Lord would help her through the evening moment by moment.

She also knew she could call her sponsor back if she needed to, anytime, day or night, just as she had made the same promise as the sponsor to a newer member of their support group.

She missed the support and camaraderie of

meetings, but Toby needed her in the evenings. When she was more confident that he felt settled and secure—and she prayed daily that it would happen—she might consider getting him a babysitter for the evening.

No, she wouldn't have a drink, but after the day she'd had, she would get into her sweatpants and grab a pint of chocolate ice cream and the most comforting devotional book she could find on her shelf.

She would allow herself to wallow for an hour, and then she would set about the task of figuring out what came next.

By the time she'd arrived for her meeting at the daycare, the regretful but determined look on Bethany Hoover's face had told her that Toby's fate there was sealed. She still sat swallowing back a nauseated feeling while Bethany ever so gently presented a litany of reasons why Toby couldn't continue at the daycare.

He'd refused to play with the other children. He'd refused to nap. He'd snatched toys from others and touched their food at lunchtime. He wouldn't use the bathroom, had had accidents and then screamed the place down if someone tried to clean him up.

"He's just been through a rough time," Grace had said with an ache in the back of her throat. "He's good with me. He really is."

"I believe he's a good little boy," Bethany had said kindly, though the determination in her eyes had never wavered.

Grace had tried to curb her resentful thoughts. She'd tried to believe that this was difficult for Bethany and that making hard but necessary choices was part of her job.

"He needs more specialized attention than we can give him at Child's Garden," Bethany had continued. "It's not fair to the other children, and it's not fair to Toby. You understand, don't you?"

Grace had told herself they were two professional women having a conversation, and she'd forced back her tears. She'd said she understood and thanked Bethany for trying.

Now Toby was tucked in and she was sitting alone trying to figure things out. As if to add to Grace's conflicted struggle, he'd been quite affectionate with her, at least in his way, patting her hand lightly while she'd read to him.

He'd asked for the book of photographs to look at before going to sleep, and she'd readily agreed, seeking to keep the fragile bond intact.

He really was a good boy who deserved so much more than life had given him in his brief years. She prayed she would be able to help him.

Now she sat in the wicker chair on the front porch with her feet curled up under her. Toby's bedroom window faced the porch, and she had left it open a crack, so she knew she would hear him if he needed anything.

The evening air was cool, as late August in Saskatchewan tended to be, so she wore a brown sweater that was more comfortable than flattering over her T-shirt. She found the cool breeze bracing though. It helped alleviate some of the anxiety that had settled in her stomach since the daycare meeting.

But even her favorite devotions and the smooth coldness of the ice cream on her tongue wasn't enough to chase away her panic. How was she going to manage everything if Toby had no place to go while she worked?

She was about to put the ice cream away and begin the hard work of deciphering what choices were available to her when an unfamiliar vehicle, a dark blue SUV, slowed down and came to a stop in front of her house.

To her dismay, just as John Bishop exited the vehicle, she noticed a dab of chocolate ice cream front and center in the middle of her peach-colored T-shirt. She pulled the sweater more tightly around her and stood up, although what she really wanted to do was sink through the porch steps and disappear.

She wasn't exactly dressed for company, and although she shouldn't care what John Bishop thought of her, especially not after the way he left her office, she did care.

But then she took note that he looked more embarrassed than she felt. He wavered on his crutches at the edge of the lawn and fidgeted. His hand reached back and squeezed his long-ish hair into a knot before letting it go again.

"How did you know where I live?" Grace mentally rolled her eyes at herself. Of all the questions she could have asked, that was what she came up with?

"I didn't," John replied. "I was just driving around and saw you sitting out here. I was too restless to settle into my room for the night.

"May I?" He gestured toward the porch, and Grace nodded, giving permission for him to come closer. She was glad for the security blan-ket of her sweater.

She wasn't afraid of John. There was some-thing too vulnerable, too *wounded*, in his eyes for that. But she was a bit afraid of not being able to sort out her own feelings. She relied on being the practical one, on being able to count on herself to make sensible decisions. She didn't like even a whisper of that being upended.

John went to balance himself on the porch rail, but Grace shook her head and said, "Wait a minute." She went into the house, put the ice cream back in the freezer and the devotional on the coffee table and came out with a folding chair and a footstool.

It was just her nature to take care of people, she told herself. She couldn't help it. But she would keep things professional, and she wouldn't offer him a beverage. The invisible line bolstered her somewhat.

"How can I help you?" she asked John after he appeared to be settled in a reasonably comfortable manner. She squirmed in her own chair as she remembered that he'd said he hadn't come looking for her on purpose.

Still, it seemed pretty clear that, for whatever reason, he was glad he had found her.

"I went back to your office after my meeting," John said, speaking slowly as if he were carefully plucking each word out of a barrel of possible choices. "But you weren't there. Renee said you had to go early to the daycare."

"That's true," Grace said cautiously. She had deliberately been sparse with the details so that Renee would have less to share. The girl was a whiz with computers and great at making people feel at home, but she had no filter when it came to sharing information.

"What else did she tell you?"

"Just that." John scratched the back of his head. "I am really glad I saw you sitting out here. I went back because I wanted to apologize for the way I behaved earlier. It's a complicated story that I don't intend to get into, but you did nothing to deserve the way I treated you. I wanted to say that I'm sincerely sorry, and I hope you'll agree to continue being my physical therapist."

"So, you do want to continue?" Grace flattened her voice and fiddled with a loose button on her sweater. She tried to ground her limbs, which felt suddenly weightless now that John had taken the time to apologize and said he wasn't going to give up on his therapy.

Or on her.

"Of course I'll continue to be your PT," she said.

Once again, the smile that softened and brought charm to his not-quite-handsome face made her want to give her best smile in return.

"Should we fist-bump?" he quipped. "Is that what the cool kids are doing these days?"

So, there was also a sense of humor behind that rugged world-weariness. She couldn't help her heart skipping in anticipation at the chance to get to know him better over the next little while.

He is your patient. Nothing more.

With the apology over, John didn't appear to be in any rush to leave, and Grace wondered if she should offer that beverage after all. Just then, an anguished moan came from Toby's bedroom window.

"Mommy!" The word was a jagged saw that ripped apart the dusky peace of the evening.

Grace started up in her chair and then couldn't help noticing that John flinched as if the cry had physically wounded him.

"He needs you," he said. His voice wobbled slightly. "You should go… I should leave." But he remained stock-still, hands gripping the sides of the chair.

"He's calling for his real mother." Grace's throat constricted. "It's better to see if he'll settle himself again. Sometimes seeing me just makes it worse."

She tried to keep the bitterness out of her voice, tried to swallow away the bile it created. It was hard, far too hard sometimes, not to wonder how a little boy could yearn so desperately for a woman who hadn't cared for even his most basic needs, let alone offered him the love and affection that every child needed and deserved.

She tried to hand those questions over to God, and sometimes she had to do it over and over again. She did know it wasn't her place to judge.

"Mommy!"

Grace stood, and John tried to push himself into a standing position as quickly as he could. She didn't doubt that he wanted to get going.

It wasn't exactly comfortable hanging around while someone else's child was upset.

But instead of making a quick exit, he asked, "Can I try to help?"

Grace looked at him speculatively, but the compassion in his eyes and the strange but undeniable sensation that he understood Toby's cry on a deeper level than she did made her trust him.

He had said that Toby reminded him of someone he used to know.

"Yes," she said. "If you think you can help, please, yes."

Chapter Four

What in the world am I doing?

There was no reason, none at all, for John to get involved in Grace's life. This woman was his physical therapist. She was his best hope of achieving his end goal of getting out of Living Skies as quickly as humanly possible.

Not only that, but he was a complete stranger to the boy. Even if Toby would rather see his real mother than Grace, she was a far better option than he was.

John told himself all of this but still hobbled behind Grace as she led him to the room where the little boy slept. He could have found it himself. The pitiful cries coming from the room provided a mournful guide.

There wasn't really time to fully take in the kind of house Grace lived in, but he got the general impression of practicality that still managed to offer warmth.

So very much like its owner.

Grace reached the room and inched the door open. The action caused the whimpering cry to cut off abruptly, but there was a shock to the silence, like a ribbon that had been too sharply sliced by scissors.

Over Grace's shoulder, John could see the soft glow emanating from a night-light and the small, skinny figure of a boy sitting up in bed clenching covers pulled up to his chin.

"Toby," Grace said softly, again exhibiting that cautious hope that John had witnessed in her office on that first day. It was so unlike her usual demeanor and conveyed such unconscious vulnerability that he wanted to reach out and offer comfort and reassurance in whatever way he could.

He would not, of course.

"Toby, this is my friend John."

Friend. The choice of word caused something that started deep within and wrapped itself around him like a warm blanket, even as he told himself that Grace had chosen the word for the ease of it. There was no need to trouble young Toby with their therapist-patient relationship.

That was the sum of their relationship.

Toby's eyes, big and round in his thin face, darted warily between them. He tugged the blanket up farther until only those eyes were showing. He reminded John so much of Simon and his perpetual unease, and for one horrifying moment, John was afraid that he was going to burst into tears.

He understood why their mother had to rescue Simon, but what he could never, ever, understand was why she hadn't been able to look past the tough exterior he presented and understand that he was just as afraid as Simon. Just because he'd had to pretend to be strong to protect his little brother didn't mean he was.

"John takes pictures," Grace said in a *tread carefully* voice. "He might like to see the pictures in your nature book."

John cleared his throat, rummaged and found his own voice. "I would like that very much. If you'd like to show me?"

He was following Grace's lead, and it seemed that asking the boy directly about his nighttime woes was not the chosen way to proceed. Then again, that made sense. Why would they ask him if he missed his mom when it was excruciatingly clear that he did, and there was nothing they could do about it?

Toby hesitated, glancing at Grace, who nodded encouragement. With a shuddering sigh, he reached under his pillow, tugged the book out and then hugged it to his chest as if unsure what to do with it.

"You'll want to sit down," Grace said. It didn't

register with John right away that she was talking to him. With his attention on Toby, he hadn't even noticed how much his ankle was throbbing.

She was back to being his PT, but in a distracted kind of way. Although she helped him into a nearby chair, it was obvious her mind wasn't on him.

And he was happy about that.

For one thing, it wouldn't be right for her to be thinking of him when she needed to be thinking about a troubled foster child. For another, he really didn't want to breathe in her fresh, clean scent for any longer than he had to. It played havoc on his pulse. So he would be grateful if she hurried to end their contact.

Now she hung back as if she were waiting for him to do something.

Of course she was waiting, John admonished himself. He had asked if he could help, which had probably led her to believe that he actually had some ideas or knew what he was doing.

Toby still clung tightly to the treasured book and looked first at Grace and then at John, waiting to see what came next.

John closed his eyes and breathed slowly in and out, calling to mind the kinds of things he would have said and done to try to soothe away Simon's fears. If he remembered correctly, it was mostly a case of trying to help Simon see past the present moment, past the circumstances that had drenched him in fear. He needed to give him something else to focus on, something to believe in.

He opened his eyes. "Toby, I'd really like it if you showed me your favorite picture and told me what you like best about it."

John watched as the expression on Toby's face turned from fear and grief to one of contemplation. He slowly began to turn the pages.

"This one." He pointed at a page. "I like this one."

"May I?"

Toby placed the book in his hands.

The photograph had captured the exact moment that an eagle was gently placing a piece of meat into its chick's mouth.

A tremor ran through John's hands, and he gripped the sides of the book and swallowed. He could sense Grace's gaze on him and glanced up. Her anxious eyes and the way she gnawed her lip told him that she also understood all too well why Toby had chosen this picture.

He wouldn't push the boy on *why* he'd chosen it. That answer would hit a bit too close to home for both of them. Instead, he began to point out various facets of the picture and explain the techniques that a photographer might use to capture that image.

Of course, John knew that Toby wouldn't understand half of it, but his goal was to give the little boy something else to think about.

When he realized that the little boy had sidled over to him and was leaning into his side listening intently, John knew that it had worked, and he exhaled a large breath.

He kept talking and explaining things in a calm, methodical way until Toby's breathing told him that the little boy had fallen asleep again.

Memories of Simon crashed through him, and he wondered if he would ever know how his little brother's life had turned out. He wished he could truly believe that God was listening when he prayed and that Simon had found safety and happiness.

"Thank you," Grace said.

John was happy for the distraction her voice provided him. "You're welcome," he said. "I'm just thankful that I was able to calm him down."

"Yes, God was with you," Grace said in such a natural, conversational way that he knew she must be one of those people who were simply able to accept that God was part of their daily lives.

The uncomfortableness that washed over him was only partially due to his ankle that screamed it needed relief. The soft glow of the night-light and the silence that had fallen between them, broken only by Toby's slightly ragged breathing, suddenly made the whole scene too intimate.

It didn't help matters that he was also all too aware of Grace's soft breathing and the way her pretty hair picked up the soft light.

John cleared his throat and pushed himself out of the chair, wincing as his foot made contact with the floor. He gritted his teeth and re-adjusted his stance.

"I'd, uh, better get going," he said.

"Yes," Grace said immediately. "Thank you so much again. I'll show you out."

Her hurried response signaled to John that she too sensed a vibe in the room that she wasn't comfortable with.

Again, he pictured himself getting into his car and just driving until he hit the next town. But then Toby sighed and turned in his sleep, and Grace's eyes went soft with relief, and John knew he couldn't just take off.

But he wasn't ready to think about exactly why that was.

Back in his motel room, sleep was an elusive goal.

He absolutely would not let his thoughts linger on Grace. He had to get any imaginings of touching her soft-looking hair or drawing her into a comforting embrace well under control before his physio appointment in the morning.

John reached for his phone, pulled up a search engine and in a habitual way typed in *Simon Bishop*. Sometimes he typed in their mother's name, *Melody Bishop*. Of course, he had no way of knowing if she had kept the Bishop name. He had every reason to believe that she would not have done so.

As always, a barrage of names flooded his screen, but it was impossible at first glance to tell if any of them had anything to do with his mother or brother.

John heaved an exasperated sigh at the hopelessness of it all. Rather than go down the futile rabbit hole of endless scrolling, he turned his phone off.

He opened the drawer in the nightstand beside the bed and pulled out the Bible that had been placed there. He hesitated for a moment and then flipped it open and began to read.

When John arrived at the clinic the next morning, Renee remarked, "You look like you had a rough night." She studied him with unabashed interest.

"I had quite a bit on my mind," John acknowledged. That was all the curious and chatty Renee was going to get out of him.

He definitely wasn't going to say anything about his impromptu visit to Grace's house last night or about how he'd helped her with her foster son. He was sure that Grace wouldn't be broadcasting the news either.

What he had said about having things on his mind was true enough. The psalms he had read to try to lull himself into sleep had at first comforted him, but then they had raised a flurry of questions. It was clear that the writers of these psalms had gone through hardships, even dangerous ones. They'd experienced the deaths of loved ones and faced many other challenging situations, including teetering dangerously on the edge of losing their own faith. Yet they'd never quite lost it. They'd kept hanging on.

How had they managed to do that? How had they kept turning to God in the midst of all of those negative things instead of rejecting Him?

It was a question that had kept John awake, along with all of the other ones racing through his mind. He hadn't found any satisfactory answers to any of them.

The way his heart skipped a beat when Grace opened the door to her office to call him in told him that there was one answer he didn't dare keep seeking.

The shadows under her eyes conveyed that she hadn't slept well either. They gave her a vulnerable look. Unfortunately, they also made her more appealing.

"How's the ankle?"

Okay, so they were going to get straight down to business.

But what else was he expecting?

"No worse," John said. "Maybe a little better."

Grace tapped her pen on her palm. It seemed to John to be an uncharacteristically nervous gesture.

He waited for her next instructions, prepared to manipulate his ankle into painful positions to show that he was making progress.

"How did you do it?" Grace asked.

"How did I…?" Her question threw him. "Are you asking *how* I did the exercises you gave me?" He began to demonstrate.

"No." The rushed word came out indisputably nonprofessional. Grace must have heard that too, because she slammed her mouth shut, and her cheeks went pink.

"I mean, I'm glad your ankle is making progress, but…" Her voice trailed off, and then she said all in a rush, "I meant, how did you get Toby to trust you?"

John's stomach clenched. He'd never said Simon's name out loud, not to anyone. He'd never been tempted to before. But he knew if he opened that lid, what spilled out would be so messy that he might never get it cleaned up.

It was bad enough that Grace knew his father—or at least thought she did. She apparently didn't want to know the truth about him.

"Believe it or not, I was once a little boy not that different from Toby," he said.

"But you weren't a foster child," Grace mused. "I know your father."

As if he needed reminding.

He wasn't going to get into a discussion about his father with someone who obviously wasn't willing to hear the truth about the man, and there was no way he was mentioning his mother or Simon.

"I guess I just meant that I know what it's like to be a little boy…and to be afraid."

"What were you afraid of?"

Grace's eyes ran over him. As practiced as her assessment was, John was sure that she still saw his injured ankle as the most vulnerable part of him.

There were so many answers to her question, but all he said was, "Oh, the usual things that kids are afraid of. I think we're all afraid of something, aren't we?"

Grace didn't answer, but her face grew thoughtful.

Grace was trying to think of a way to get some nutrients into Toby's body in a way that he wouldn't kick up a fuss. Mac and cheese was always a hit, but he couldn't live on just that. But when she tried to add veggies to it, no matter how finely they were chopped, Toby always noticed and balked at eating it.

She'd heard of some people substituting cauliflower for the pasta, but she couldn't imagine Toby falling for that one. Maybe he would eat a vegetarian lasagna if she doused it in enough sauce?

I think we're all afraid of something, aren't we?

Why couldn't she stop thinking about that? Was it because John had worded it in the present tense, which she was sure was just a slip of the tongue, or because he hadn't really answered her question?

Well, whatever it was, it was her fault for bringing up a personal subject in the first place. She wasn't going to do that again. She'd never been tempted to get close to a client before, and she was sure that this foolishness would pass. Especially since John had made it abundantly clear that he wanted to hit the road as soon as he could.

With a sigh, Grace turned back to idly flipping the pages of a cookbook, hoping that a solution to the supper dilemma would present itself. When Toby heaved out his own sigh, she turned her attention to him.

He had spent the day with Carol Barker, Pastor Liam's wife. Although Toby had claimed to have had a good time when Grace picked him up, he was now hunched in a kitchen chair, and his downturned mouth told another story.

"Hey, what's wrong, bud?"

Instantly, he sat straighter and grabbed the front of his T-shirt, twisting it.

"Nothin'," he mumbled. "I'm good. See." He jumped up and stood with his arms crossed, his defiant expression poorly masking the fear.

Grace went to him and bent down, taking both of his hands in hers.

"I can see that everything isn't okay, Toby," she said, being very careful to make sure that it sounded like an invitation, not an accusation. "If you tell me what it is, I'm sure I can help."

Please, Lord, let that be true.

"Did you not have a good time with Mrs. Barker? I'm so sorry. I promise I'll find you a place where you will have other nice kids to play with as soon as I can."

Of course, she hadn't told Toby why he was being removed from Child's Garden Daycare. There was no way in the world that she would say or do anything to make the little boy think it was his fault. Inwardly, she still seethed in a maybe not-so-Christian way at their lack of understanding and patience, although her practical side could see that they didn't really have a choice. As Bethany had said, they simply weren't equipped to support Toby's unique needs.

The trouble was finding a place that could.

"Mrs. Barker is nice," Toby said.

"Then, what is it?" Grace urged.

Before Toby could answer, his small stomach let out a surprisingly large rumble. It would have been comical, except Grace swallowed sorrow when she realized what it meant:

Toby was hungry, and he was afraid to tell her.

There was absolutely no evidence that Toby's mother had abused him in a physical way, but Grace knew how easy it was for an addiction to become a full-time preoccupation, making a person unaware or unwilling to deal with anything else. She wondered how many nights Toby had gone to bed hungry, learning to repress his own needs because he didn't want to be a bother.

Grace longed to gather him into her arms, but she knew he would cringe away. Instead, she offered her hand. After a moment's hesitation, he took it, and she led him to sit beside her on the couch. She turned to him with all the reassurance she could muster in her voice and smile.

"Toby, I'm going to tell you something, and I want you to listen carefully. Can you do that for me?"

He nodded, but his expression didn't warm, and she made herself push aside the question of whether it ever would. Now was not the time.

"If you are ever hungry, or if there is ever anything you need or want, I want you to tell me right away, day or night, got it?"

Toby nodded, but his eyes shifted away from hers.

"I'll tell you what," Grace continued, determined that she wouldn't show the little boy her worry that she would never truly get through to him. "You know the cupboard beside the stove? The one I told you is called a lazy Susan, that when you pull it out, the shelves spin so you can see what's on them?"

Toby nodded solemnly.

"Well, from now on, I'll make sure there are always good snacks in there that you can get if you are hungry and I'm slow making supper, okay? I'll also keep a bowl of fruit out that you can help yourself to whenever you want. How does that sound?"

"Good," Toby said softly, and a whisper of relief came into his eyes.

Perhaps offering snacks in between meals wasn't the best long-term fix, but Grace didn't care if it meant making progress with Toby.

She settled on hamburgers for supper and managed to sneak in some vitamins with a sliced tomato garnish, which Toby thankfully ate without comment. She wondered if he would eat veggies if she got some dip for them and made a mental note to pick some up.

Grace tidied up the kitchen while Toby played in some sudsy water at the sink. She had dealt with a problem and made some strides with him, and she thanked God for it.

Her relief, however, turned out to be short-lived.

When Grace tucked Toby in and began to say their usual bedtime prayer, instead of folding his hands, he folded his arms in a stubborn gesture across his chest and said with a kind of belligerence she hadn't heard from him before, "I'm not gonna say prayers with you. You're not my mom."

Grace's chest tightened. It wasn't unusual for Toby to pull back if something happened to cause him to feel that he'd been disloyal to his own mother. Still, she clenched her jaw in frustration.

She wanted to tell him it wasn't disloyal to be hungry or to be thankful he had something to eat.

What would John tell him? What would he tell me to do?

No, she wasn't going to resort to that. There was no point getting into a habit that was destined to be short-lived.

"Okay," Grace said in a calm, nonreactive way. "We don't have to say prayers tonight, but if there's anything you want to talk to God about, you can just think about it and He'll hear you."

Toby rotated his mouth, thinking. "Is that true?" he asked her.

Grace nodded. "Absolutely one hundred percent true."

The room was silent for a moment while Toby pondered this.

"Would you like one of your books to look at?" Grace offered.

"Can John come over and talk to me about the pictures again?"

Grace wanted to say he couldn't. The night before had been unplanned and unexpected. There were too many reasons to count why it wasn't good for either Toby or Grace to get in the habit of counting on another person, particularly one who wasn't going to be around for long.

Deep within, in a place she wasn't willing to explore yet, and probably never would be, Grace sensed that her instinct to push John away wasn't just for Toby's sake. She was a recovering addict, and she would always be an addict. Keeping that secret from most people meant keeping up a wall that was so firmly entrenched that Grace usually didn't even think about it being there.

That was until someone like John Bishop came along and unwittingly created an atmosphere of partnership, teamwork and trust that she only dared to long for in the most hidden recesses of her heart.

Aside from all that, there was Toby, hugging his favorite book to his chest. In his pale blue eyes, defiance and hope dwelled side by side.

So instead of giving the firm no that Grace knew would be the best answer, she heard herself saying, "It's bedtime for you, and we can't expect Mr. Bishop to just drop whatever he's doing and come over. But maybe I could give him a call or talk to him soon, and see if he could spend more time with you."

Dear Lord, what am I getting myself into?

It was hard to think about the possible repercussions with Toby's eyes shining at her like that.

"Do you want me to read your book to you?" Grace offered.

Toby shook his head. "Uh-uh," he said. "I'll read it to myself."

"Okay then…have a good night. I love you, Toby," Grace added.

As she eased the door shut, she heard him murmuring, "Now, the photog-affer sometimes has to wait for the right light, so it takes a lotta pay-shunce."

It brought back a picture of John and Toby huddled over the book, almost like they belonged together.

The next morning, after a fitful night, Grace poured herself a large cup of coffee. Resigned to the fact that sleep was going to elude her, she'd decided to be productive with her time and do some more online research for a day-care that had both the space and the expertise to accommodate Toby. It was a given that she'd be looking at a commute, because she'd already exhausted the best of Living Skies' formal child-care options.

As she scanned the facilities' overviews, Grace took slow, deep breaths, determined not to succumb to panic. She knew she was looking not just for a place that would be able to deal with the little boy on a clinical level but one that would truly welcome him and believe that he was a child with as much potential as any other.

She wondered what John meant when he said that he was once a little boy not unlike Toby. Well, she had her secrets, and he had his, and that's the way things would remain.

It was a logical conclusion, so why did her heart feel like it was shriveling up in disappointment?

Her disappointment at the situation with John soon transferred over to the research she was doing. The schools she found were either too clinical-sounding for her tastes or they had no openings and at least a two-year waiting list.

She clicked out of the sites and picked up her Bible, regretful that she hadn't started with that. Ultimately, the way things turned out was in God's hands. She would just have to keep reminding herself of that truth.

"Is it time for school?" Toby's sleepy voice startled Grace.

He stood in the doorway of her office, and the sight of him rubbing his sleep-tinged eyes and his bedhead made her all the more determined to find a place where he would be nurtured in the way he most needed.

"No, I'm sorry if I woke you," Grace said. "I just got up early to get a little bit of extra work done. Do you want something to eat?"

Toby put two fingers in his mouth and shook his head. His pajama bottoms drooped dangerously low, and he tugged them up with his other hand.

"Are you sure?" Grace prodded gently, mindful of the previous night's occurrence.

Toby considered. "Is there cereal?"

"There sure is." Grace closed her Bible and stood up.

She went to the kitchen to pour him a bowl of cereal, and while she was topping it with milk, Toby asked, "Can we phone Mr. Bissup?"

"It's too early," Grace answered. "He'll still be sleeping."

But as she said it, she could suddenly picture John being awake. Maybe because it was easy to assume that his ankle would be bothering him, but more because she could imagine that as a photographer, he would be inclined to get up early to catch the day as it began to unfold. Or because he had a lot of things on his mind or…

What am I doing speculating on his sleep habits?

While Toby ate his cereal, Grace poured herself another cup of coffee and popped a piece of bread into the toaster for herself.

"When will I go to school today?" Toby asked. Grace took a sip of coffee and swallowed.

"You're going to Mrs. Barker's house today again. Won't that be fun?"

She had decided to take things one day at a time and not offer Toby a full explanation about why he wasn't going to Child's Garden anymore. She prayed that she would find a better alternative and then would simply be able to say that he was being moved to a place where he'd have more fun.

It was interesting that he had been acting out

extensively at Child's Garden, yet he expected to go there and was probably having a hard time figuring out why he wasn't. Grace reasoned that it was probably because it was easier for people—especially for someone like Toby—to gravitate to what was familiar, even if it wasn't what was best for him.

Toby nodded, but there was no life in his expression.

Grace continued to puzzle over his reactions to things. According to Bethany, he'd acted out in a borderline aggressive manner at the daycare, while with her, he was docile to the point of being void of emotion.

She couldn't help but think of the way his face had lit up with genuine curiosity and excitement as John had flipped through the pages of the book with him. Once again, her heart urged her that a surefire way to make a real connection with Toby was to have John be a part of their lives.

Toby's life, not my life.

But that was a ridiculous thought. It was. John had made it very clear that he didn't want to be in Living Skies.

Nonetheless, the stubborn and determined part of Grace reared its head, telling her that he was here now.

Chapter Five

If John had been asked to make a list of a hundred or even a thousand things he thought he might be doing on a Friday afternoon, having lunch in the park with his PT and her foster son would not have even crossed his mind.

He didn't even have another appointment scheduled with Grace until Monday. She had given him a series of exercises to work through at their last appointment and had said it would be best to let him work on them for a few days before making another assessment.

He had told himself it was silly to be disappointed.

Then this morning, while he was spreading butter on a muffin from the small stash of groceries he'd picked up for his room, he'd realized that his first thought upon waking hadn't been of how much his ankle hurt but of how good that muffin was going to taste.

His second thought had been of Grace, which

was maybe why the realization that his ankle was starting to feel better wasn't filling him with the relief he'd thought it would.

That was not a good thing.

After breakfast, John tidied up and then found himself reaching for the Bible again. It was the oddest thing. He was far from being ready to stake his life on what he was reading, but he couldn't stop thinking about it...even if his eyes wanted to skim over the parts on forgiveness.

He wouldn't ever believe that God wanted him to forgive his father.

When the phone in the room rang, it startled him. He considered not answering because it flashed into his mind that it might be his father. But then the next thought was that it could be Stew Wagner calling again about *The Chronicle*. Somehow, John was no longer sure that he could automatically dismiss the opportunity.

He couldn't stay in Living Skies, of course. Not while his father was here flaunting his new image and probably thinking they were going to have some kind of do-over. But working remotely might be a good option.

When Grace's voice answered his hello, John told himself that it was only the surprise of it that caused the shiver of anticipation to run up his spine.

"Toby really wants to see you again," she said,

coming right to the point with anxiousness and something else in her voice that he couldn't quite decipher.

She went on to briefly explain that she had taken the afternoon off work because there were some things going on with Toby's daycare and he especially needed her these days.

And Toby needed him too?

Everything within John shouted that this was too much. Sharing the goal of making a child's life better created a bond between them that couldn't possibly exist because they barely knew one another.

"Would you like me to come over, or do you want me to meet you somewhere?" he asked, ignoring the inner voice that had taken pretty good care of him up to this point.

That was how John found himself in Caledon Park, sitting on a plaid blanket, eating chicken salad sandwiches, carrot sticks and chocolate chip cookies and washing it down with lemonade.

It reminded him of the kind of lunches that children took to school…not that he'd ever had that kind of lunch.

Truth be known, it was a bit on the cool side for a picnic. The breeze that played with Grace's hair in an appealing way had the whisper of autumn about it.

"I know some people wouldn't consider this ideal picnic weather," Grace said, as if she knew what he was thinking, "but ever since I was a kid, I haven't been able to stand being too hot."

"I like this kind of weather too," John said.

"You must have experienced all different kinds in your travels."

"Yes, I sure have."

Grace leaned slightly toward him with her eyes shining, another question poised on her lips.

"Oh!" Toby cried out in surprise as lemonade splashed out of his cup and down the front of his shirt.

Watching Grace's face was like watching a book fall open to the page that told all of its secrets. John knew that she wanted to assure the boy that he wasn't in trouble, but her face also showed she was dismayed at letting their conversation distract her.

She cleaned Toby up as well as she could, murmuring reassurances, and when she turned back to John, her next words were about the boy. That wasn't a surprise, so why did he feel weighed down with disappointment?

Toby's resemblance to John's brother, Simon, drew him in and created an instant bond, but that didn't mean it wouldn't have been enjoyable to share some of his favorite travel anecdotes with Grace. He knew she would be a keen and perceptive listener. Not that he was trying to impress her, not a chance.

"Toby brought the book with him," Grace said. "He was hoping he could ask you a few more questions."

"Of course you can, Toby." John was careful to direct his gaze to the boy's eager face. He couldn't make sense of what, if anything, Grace wanted from him.

Maybe she didn't know either.

He almost envied Toby his innocent oblivion over the unspoken tension between the adults. Then again, maybe the tension was only in his mind. Grace had leaped to her feet and seemed fully preoccupied with shaking crumbs off the blanket and folding it.

"I can help you with cleaning up," John offered.

"No," she answered almost too quickly. "You just sit with Toby." Then, almost like an afterthought, she asked, "How is your ankle feeling?"

It was strange and rather telling that they hadn't even mentioned his ankle up to that point, even though that was supposed to be the only reason they had anything at all to do with one another.

"It's okay," he answered automatically. He realized that he hadn't been thinking of it whatsoever and had to focus on it to see if what he'd answered was true. There was some discomfort, but nothing even close to as bad as it had been.

Somehow he wasn't as eager for Grace to know that as he had been at the start.

"I'm still not overdoing things," he added.

She nodded. "That's probably a good idea. Of course, we'll get a full assessment when I see you on Monday."

His heart ping-ponged like she was referring to a future date. He really had to get a grip on whatever it was that was happening to him.

"We could sit there." Grace pointed to a picnic table close to where they'd spread out the blanket.

They settled on one of the benches, and John asked, "Okay, what have you got?"

As Toby pointed at the pictures and asked questions, John was struck by two things. The first was that the little boy had a very good memory for what he'd already been told. The second was that he asked surprisingly astute questions about color and composition.

Of course, he didn't know that was what he was doing. He just wanted to know why the green blade of grass looked good beside the caterpillar's open, hungry mouth.

John also sensed that Grace was picking up

on Toby's perceptions too. She busied herself with tidying as long as she could but then gravitated toward them. She sat almost gingerly on the bench across from them, leaning in and nodding at Toby's questions and tossing in a few of her own.

John was nurtured by the warmth in her proud smile. He tried not to think about the way the sun shone on her hair and the way her light scent made him think of the promises of more summers to come even though this one was drawing to a close.

"Have you ever thought of buying him a camera?" John asked.

Grace's widened eyes showed she was surprised at the question.

"He's a little young, don't you think?" John could tell by the intrigued tone in her voice that she wasn't ready to completely dismiss the idea.

"I'm not thinking anything fancy," John explained. "Maybe one of those little disposable cameras? I think they still sell those, even though everyone just takes pictures on their phones now."

He shuddered in an exaggerated perish-the-thought kind of way, and Grace's peal of laughter was like hearing his favorite song for the first time.

"Do you really think he could handle it?" she asked with cautious hope.

"With your help, I don't see why not," John answered. "He's obviously interested, and he seems to have the right eye for photography already. I started a lot later, but who knows what could have happened if I'd had someone to encourage me at an earlier age."

He cut himself off. He wasn't going to start divulging information about his pathetic past.

He knew that Grace would catch the hesitation as easily as a bird catching the wind, but he also saw her make the decision not to push.

He wondered if she knew how readable her face was…and how easy it was to trust her because of it.

"We could go look for one now," he suggested. "I'd be happy to get one for Toby."

"Get me what?" Toby asked, turning his head from one adult to the other.

This time, it was Grace's turn to hesitate. "I'm not sure that's such a good idea."

"Why? Because you don't want Toby to have his own camera, or because you don't want me to get it for him?"

"My own camera?" Toby piped up excitedly.

Grace leveled a look at him. "Apparently," she said in a low voice, "you haven't heard that kids develop supersonic hearing if their names are mentioned in connection with getting something."

"I doubt that's happened for Toby very often," John said. He immediately regretted his words when he saw Grace's eyes dim like there was a blind being pulled down to shut out the light. He already knew how much she worried about not being able to gain the boy's full trust, and the last thing he wanted was to cause her more guilt. "I just meant…"

"I know what you meant." Grace plucked a little at the skin on the back of her hand, looking thoughtful. She raised her head and looked searchingly at him.

"Do you really think it's a good idea? I mean, I wouldn't let you pay for it. I couldn't do that. But do you think a camera might…help Toby?"

"It helped me," John said, choosing to be direct. "It still helps me. But you're Toby's guardian, and it's your call. I didn't mean to imply in any way that you aren't already doing everything you can to help him cope."

Grace grimaced a little and tilted her head toward Toby, who was still listening carefully, probably hoping to hear the word *camera* again.

John drew a zipper across his mouth, apologizing with his eyes.

He really did have a lot to learn about children, but was he going to commit himself to doing so?

No, he wasn't. He had to hit the road. He needed to get back to his life, to the place where he didn't wake up thinking about a foster child that made him miss his brother. And the child's guardian… Well, she just made him miss things he pretended he didn't want.

"Toby," Grace said, "can you please be a helper and carry the picnic basket to the car?"

Toby's reluctance showed as he removed himself from between them on the bench, but he did what she asked nevertheless.

When he was out of earshot, Grace said in a hushed, hurried voice. "I appreciate what you're trying to do here, and I will give it some thought. But I just… Well, there's just so much…"

Her voice and chin wobbled, and John longed to comfort her with a hug.

Seconds later, though, she regained a grip on herself. "I'm not doing nearly as well with Toby as you think."

The anxiety in her eyes belied her careful delivery.

John knew that he needed to tread carefully. He wanted to take a step forward, but what that step meant, he didn't know.

"Is there something you want to talk about?" he asked.

* * *

John Bishop was her patient. He wasn't a counselor. He wasn't her boyfriend. He wasn't even her friend. He was someone she was treating for an injured ankle. That was it. End of story.

Okay, granted, he was also someone who had an uncanny knack for bonding with the same little boy who she struggled to connect with, and that wasn't something that was easy to dismiss.

She told herself that was the reason she was going to open up to him. It had nothing to do with his warm and steady gaze, or with the fact that he gave off an aura of strength and protection.

There was no way she needed his protection.

Still, everyone could use a listening ear sometimes.

"I wouldn't mind," Grace said, "but there's still Toby. I don't want him to hear any of this."

John scratched his chin thoughtfully. Some stubble had sprouted there, and Grace found it more attractive than she wanted to.

"Could you take Toby to his daycare? Do they let kids come for half days?"

Grace swallowed. Her throat ached.

"That's part of the problem," she said. "Or at least, it's the part of the problem that's made me think about how badly I'm handling some other problems."

John furrowed his brow questioningly, but she shook her head, already regretting that she'd said that much.

"You're not handling anything badly," John said as easily as if she'd just told him that she preferred oranges to apples. "Toby is a great kid, but I can guess he can be challenging."

Grace looked anxiously in the little boy's direction. Fortunately, he was preoccupied dragging a small stick to make patterns in some dirt near the car. "We really can't talk about this here," she reminded John.

"But I think we should talk about it."

Grace folded her arms and looked up at him. She was tall, and with her athletic build, she didn't feel petite around many men. Even leaning on his crutches, John was an intimidating presence. But when she saw his eyes, awareness flashed through her. He did understand Toby, for whatever reason.

Had he been abused or neglected as a child? She thought of the George Bishop she knew now, and it didn't seem possible. She knew he was an alcoholic and that alcohol could enter a person's system like a poison and twist them into someone they never meant to be. But faith and great determination could also change someone.

George was an example of that, and she hoped that she was too.

"Why are you so anxious to help?" she asked, unable to resist voicing the question.

John's eyes closed for a moment, and his mouth tightened. "Toby reminds me of someone I used to know, someone I wished I could have helped more at the time."

"Was it someone you knew well?" Grace sensed she was pushing a boundary, but since she had escaped the shadow of alcohol herself, straightforward communication was important to her. Of course, that didn't mean she shared her own experience as an alcoholic with many people. She didn't believe there was a lot to be gained by doing so. But she had always promised herself that if anyone came right out and asked her if she was an alcoholic, she would be truthful. She simply didn't volunteer the information.

John met her gaze steadily, but his face remained unyielding.

"You could say that."

It was clear she wasn't going to get anything else out of him, and they couldn't continue this conversation while Toby hung around the car. She noticed he was watching them again.

She reminded herself that the only reason they were together today in the first place was because Toby had expressed an interest in seeing John again. She was doing this so she could learn ways to connect with the boy, not to use John as a sounding board for issues she should be figuring out on her own.

"Well, this has been great," she said. "Thank you for spending time with Toby. I will consider the camera idea," she added. Her voice sounded stilted to her own ears, like they were in a formal negotiation.

Apparently, John heard it too, because his mouth quirked in an odd way that made it difficult to tell if he was amused or annoyed.

Maybe a little of both.

"So, that's it?" he asked. "We're just going to pretend that there isn't something you really need to talk about?"

Grace squinted her eyes and tugged at a piece of her hair.

"At the very least," John said, "let me treat Toby to a camera. Nothing expensive, I promise."

Why was he being so persistent about this?

She didn't want any kind of tension in their appointments, and if talking to John would help Toby in any way, which was her main goal in this, she should agree to it.

"I'll make a quick call to someone," she said before she had a chance to change her mind.

"I'll see if Toby can spend an hour with them so we can get this talked out and…" she heaved a sigh, unable to believe she was giving in on this so easily "…you can get a camera for him. But," she added, raising a finger against John's satisfied grin, "nothing fancy."

A little while later, Toby was dropped off at Pastor Liam and Carol Barker's house, and Grace found herself surveying a display of inexpensive cameras at Lloyd's Local Drugstore.

Unsure of what she was looking for, she glanced over at John and saw that he was using his crutches only casually. His weight was distributed almost evenly between the leg with the injured ankle and the one without.

It appeared that John Bishop was a fast healer. *Why wasn't she happier about that?*

"You're putting weight on your ankle," she said, glad that she still managed to sound clinical and observational despite the drumbeat of uncertainty that thumped through her.

John glanced down. "Hmm, I guess I am. It hurts less when I let myself get distracted by other things."

Like what things? Grace wanted to ask him, but being tempted to hint for compliments for no good reason was being foolish. Besides, it was clear that he was just a nice guy who wanted to do something for Toby.

She turned her attention back to the cameras, which were the only reason they were shopping together in the first place.

"What do you recommend?" she asked.

John reached up and lifted a small camera down from the display. He turned it over in his hands, looking at it before he handed it to her.

"It's not disposable," he said, "but I think it's a good price. It might be better for Toby to have something he can keep and use. I just have the feeling he's going to take to photography…the way I did."

"He's still just a little boy," Grace reminded John, "and you don't really know him, even if you say that he reminds you of someone."

She secretly hoped that the unspoken question would encourage John to reveal more about himself and his background.

"You're in charge," he said. "We'll do whatever you feel is best."

A few minutes later, Grace was at the cash register paying for the camera that John had recommended. She wouldn't have felt right buying something for Toby that was made to be impermanent and discarded. Not even in the smallest way did she want anything to symbolize that he wasn't worth a lifetime commitment of love and care.

As they were exiting the store, they almost bumped into Bethany Hoover.

"Oh!" the daycare director said, startled. "Hello, Grace." Her eyes swept over John, and there was clearly curiosity in them.

"I see you're out and about, which must mean you've been able to make arrangements for Toby. I'm so glad."

"Temporary arrangements," Grace said with a smile that felt more like she was gritting her teeth. She knew she was being petty, but she didn't want Bethany to forget that she hadn't left them in an easy position.

The part of her that fought a daily battle to be more like Jesus spoke up in a quiet voice to say that Bethany simply had a job to do and was trying her best to manage everything as best she could.

Grace deliberately softened her tone and facial muscles. "Toby is with Carol Barker while I run some errands. But I'm sure we'll be able to find more permanent arrangements for him soon."

As she spoke, Grace watched Bethany's eyes flit back and forth between her and John. She was clearly waiting for an introduction...or an explanation, but Grace had no desire to oblige.

"Good to see you, Bethany, but if you'll excuse me, I have to pick up Toby. I promised him I wouldn't be long."

It had taken all her willpower not to say "*we* have to pick up Toby."

"What was that all about?" John asked as they went to Grace's car.

She thought for a moment about pretending she didn't know what he was talking about.

"Your mouth was smiling, but your eyes sure weren't," he added.

It made her feel exposed and vulnerable when John made observations like that. But, of course, that was probably what made him an exceptional photographer. He had an innate ability for ob-servation. It was nothing personal.

She would do her best not to wish that it was.

Grace wasn't sure what was happening to her. She had always been focused on her career, sat-isfied with her single life and didn't often feel like there was anything lacking. She had always been one to believe that there were many ways to have a fulfilling life, and that it didn't have to include romantic love.

Now she wondered if all that was an excuse to keep anyone from getting too close, because that would mean having to share her secret.

"You're not answering," John prodded, but in a gentle way. "I think I've overstepped a boundary."

Grace shook her head. "That was the director

of Toby's daycare. Well, the daycare he used to go to before they decided he was too disruptive."

"Toby?" John wrinkled his brow. "He doesn't seem like a rabble-rouser to me. He's more attentive than most kids I know, not that I have a lot of experience."

"He's good with you," Grace said. "He likes you. But Toby…" She paused, taking a deep breath of air into a heavy feeling in her chest. "He does have some issues. They're not his fault," she added hurriedly. "But he does need more than the daycare can offer. I'm trying not to be mad at Bethany. Logically, I know she made the only decision she could make, but…"

"But it's hard to be logical when you care so much about someone," John said.

They had reached the car. Grace darted a glance up at him. He wasn't looking at her though. He was looking into the distance as if searching for something.

"I'd better drop you off and pick up Toby," she said after a moment. "I promised Carol I wouldn't be long."

"Could I come with you?" John asked tentatively. "I'd love to see his reaction when you give him the camera. I could give him a few pointers too."

Grace was about to say that she was sure that she could show Toby how to point and click, but then she noticed John's eyes. His expression was vulnerable and…lonely.

But it wasn't like he didn't know anyone in Living Skies. She didn't usually let her curiosity get the best of her, but she couldn't resist asking, "Do you think you'll spend any time with your father while you're here?"

"No." John's sharp retort crushed her question almost before she finished asking it. His face hardened, and she noticed him flexing his fingers and taking deep breaths as if to try to calm himself. "Besides," he said, his voice quieter, "you said yourself that I'm healing faster than you expected."

Grace hadn't exactly said that, but she knew what the implication was. He wanted to flee Living Skies as soon as he could.

She suspected now that his goal had something to do with his father—or maybe it was completely about his father. But the George Bishop she knew was Christian in both word and action. It was difficult for her to believe that there wasn't some way the rift between them could be mended.

"I don't know what happened between you and your father," she began tentatively, "but I know him, and he's a good man. He's one of the best I've met."

John's bitter laughter was like a lash, and

Grace took a physical step back to avoid its sting.

"I know you think you know my father, Grace," he said after they had belted themselves in and she started the car, "but you don't."

Her hands gripped the steering wheel, and she looked out at the rows of cars in the parking lot. "May I ask what he did that was so wrong that you can't get past it?"

The pause before John answered seemed endless. "He loved alcohol more than anything or anyone, and if you think that doesn't leave scars... Well, all I can say is that it does."

The secret Grace kept screamed so loudly inside of her head she feared for a moment that she might blurt something out.

Instead, she wriggled the tension out of her shoulders and eased the car into Reverse.

"I'll drop you off at the motel," she said. She thought that her voice sounded enough like her own not to raise questions.

John simply nodded, no longer insisting on the idea that he come along to show Toby the camera.

Regret gnawed Grace's stomach. She wished that she had left well enough alone and hadn't pushed on the subject of his father.

As she drove, a song on a Christian radio station filled the silence and reminded her that God was a mighty fortress. Grace wondered if maybe she should relinquish John's care to another PT.

Because if he knew the role that alcohol had played in her own life, he wouldn't want her anywhere near him.

Chapter Six

A week had passed since John and Grace had
shared the enjoyable and—yes, John admitted—
bonding picnic with Toby. Unfortunately, the
pleasant encounter had ended when he let the
emotions that were tied to his father get the best
of him.

He really strove not to do that. He fought a
hard battle not to remain a small, scared boy
and to grow into a man who knew the kind of
person he wanted to be and to live the kind of
life he wanted to live.

He canceled his next appointment with Grace,
but he was determined to keep today's, if for no
other reason than to apologize…again.

True, he wished that she would stop insisting
that his father was a good man, but he knew she
wasn't a malicious person. He also still needed
her.

For my ankle, that's all.

As much as he tried to fight it, and as much

as he tried to deny it, he couldn't help but be curious about what Grace liked so much about his father. A very small and grudging part of him had to admit that it didn't make sense to instinctively trust her but then to let that trust fall away when she expressed an opinion that he didn't agree with.

He didn't know if he would ever be willing to acknowledge that his father could have changed, but he could at least show Grace enough courtesy to listen, as long as she didn't expect him to mend fences with his father.

There were just some fences that couldn't be mended.

John splashed water on his face and looked at his reflection. He studied the eyes that had looked old to him since he was about ten years old. He thoughtfully scratched the left side of his jaw. It had been a while since he'd given himself a thorough shave. Although he never let it go long enough for a full beard to come in, the stubble was definitely substantial.

Grace had never seen him completely clean-shaven. She would probably be surprised.

The phone in his room rang, startling him. He mused wryly that it was a good thing that he hadn't started shaving yet.

John's hand froze in the air just as he was about to answer. What if it was his father? But then he recalled that he had asked the front desk to check with him before transferring any calls for that very reason.

"Hello, John here."

"Vivian Russell is on the phone for you," the young man working the front desk said.

"Oh, great, thank you," John said, wondering what Vivian could be calling about.

The idea of seeing what he could do to get *The Chronicle* back on its feet still lingered. He had to be careful though. Between that and his soft spot for Toby—and if he was honest, for Toby's guardian—he might just be in danger of getting stuck in Living Skies.

No, he would never let that happen. His father was here. The nerve-curdling memories still outweighed any good ones he had or any new ones he might make.

"Good morning, John," Vivian said. Her bright, crisp voice made him picture her pouring a cup of that horrible but oddly irresistible coffee and waiting for it to cool while she tapped a sharpened pencil on her desk.

"Do you have time to chat?" she asked.

John glanced at his watch. His appointment with Grace was in forty-five minutes.

"I have some time, sure," he said while thinking that shaving might have to wait for another

day. "I have an appointment to check the progress on my ankle this morning."

"Well, I'll get right to the point, then. I was
talking to Stew last night, and he says that if
you agree to take the reins, he can speak to the
guys who hold the purse about upping the pay.
He also wants me to remind you that you'd have
complete autonomy on the photographs you take
and the copy that goes with them."

Stew may be retired, but his influence and impact would last as long as the man drew breath
and probably longer.

"You and Stew both know it's never been
about the money," John said.

"I'm just telling you what he said," Vivian replied. John could picture her giving one of those
palms-up "don't shoot the messenger" gestures.

He wondered, what would his first story be
if he stayed? What—or who—would he want
to take pictures of?

The faces of Grace and Toby floated into his
mind, followed by his father's face, which reminded him that the reasons he'd left were still
stronger than any reason he had to stay.

"I just don't know, Vivian," he said. "I'm not
trying to be difficult. You know I think so much
of Stew that I'd do the job for free if I thought
I could wholly commit to it. The truth is, I just
don't plan on staying here in Living Skies, and

once I'm on the road again, I will want to be focused on other things."

There was a slight pause on the other end of the phone.

"Vivian?" John said. "Don't be mad at me, okay?" He didn't know Vivian well but he liked what he did know.

"I'm not mad, John," Vivian said. "I'm not even disappointed." She chuckled at the cliché. "But I sure do hope you aren't dismissing this small-town life because you think there are bigger and better things out there."

John exhaled a sigh after the call, his mind racing. Maybe Vivian had a point. He realized that although they had not been acquainted when he lived in Living Skies, because of their age difference and having no reason to be in each other's company, Vivian must know of his father's past.

On the way to his appointment, he distracted himself from being nervous about seeing Grace by seeking a story idea that was enticing enough to make him want to stay. Even though he really could do the job from anywhere, he also knew that if he committed to *The Chronicle*, he'd be committing to the whole town. It would be saying he belonged...

An angry flush spread through his body at the thought of how difficult his father had made it for him to make simple decisions. Maybe he should write an exposé on his childhood and let people—Grace—know what life with good old George had really been like.

But a moment later, he pushed the idea away.

He didn't always feel much of a connection with God these days, except through nature, but he knew enough to know that savoring the bitter taste of a grudge was no way to live. That was not the kind of person he wanted to be.

It was not the kind of person he wanted Grace to think he was.

What he wanted was to protect her and Toby. Grace might think she knew John's father and could trust him, but she was wrong.

John knew from vast experience that sometimes George Bishop could keep up the facade for an almost admirable amount of time, but it would eventually crack. At best, he might con her out of some money. At worst, he might actually harm her.

John swallowed hard, and his pulse raced just thinking about it.

No, he was not going to allow that to happen. If he wanted to be someone whose advice Grace would listen to, though, he would have to be someone that she could trust, at least enough to listen to him as far as his father was concerned. But he would have to stay long enough to make that happen. Maybe he would take Stew up on his offer and think of the story he most wanted to tell.

In the waiting room at the clinic, his thoughts continued. Obviously he couldn't continue to live at the motel. He'd have to see if there was a place somewhere he could sublet with an open lease. There would still be the issue of avoiding his father…

"Hey, I like that mountain man look you've got going on." Renee's voice interrupted his thoughts, and John looked up, slightly startled.

She touched her chin. "You're getting serious about that beard. I like it."

John touched his chin self-consciously. He really had meant to shave, but he wasn't going to get into that with Renee. Besides, Renee was not the one he wanted compliments from. He was just grateful that the waiting room wasn't jammed with people.

Grace stepped out of her office then. She looked tall, strong, clean and professional. She seemed wholly put together until her eyes met his, and then he saw the thread of anxiety woven through them.

Once the door had closed behind them in her office, they both said, "I'm sorry."

Grace blushed—actually blushed—and John's

heart melted like a sentimental snowman under a beaming sun.

"Please let me go first," she said. "I overstepped my boundaries by pushing you on the subject of your father. I shouldn't have done it, and for that, I want to apologize."

"And I shouldn't have reacted so immaturely," John said, eager to smooth it all over and then to forget about it. "I'm sorry."

"Truce?" Grace extended her hand, and when they shook, an electrical current tingled up John's arm. Then Grace tucked a stray tendril of hair behind her ear and became all business again.

John didn't know if he was relieved or disappointed that things had so rapidly returned to normal.

He sat on the examining table and held his breath while she gently prodded his ankle, not because it hurt—he was hardly paying any attention to it at all. He just didn't want to linger on the delicate peach scent of whatever shampoo she used. Whatever it was, it definitely made her hair shiny and…

Okay, Bishop, you're not exactly doing a stellar job of not thinking about it.

He winced in embarrassment, and Grace quickly drew her hand away. "Does that hurt?"

Was there concern in her voice that maybe

went just a little beyond what a PT would feel for a regular patient?

Even though that was probably just wishful thinking on his part, John considered playing it up a little. But no. That would be foolish.

Grace stepped back, folded her arms and studied him. "Is something still the matter?" she asked.

"No, not at all," John said quickly.

Grace looked for a moment like she wanted to ask more, but instead, she turned her eyes to his chart, made a note and closed it.

"Your ankle is looking good," she said. "You're a fast healer. I think that as long as you don't overdo it, it would be fine for you to start regular activity again." She paused. "In other words—" there was a waver in her voice so slight that John couldn't be sure that he hadn't just imagined it "—I don't think you are going to be stuck here as long as you were afraid of."

John was silent. He studied his hands. He didn't know how to answer a question that hadn't been asked. Instead, he lifted his head and said, "How did Toby like the camera?"

As if a light had been switched on or a stage curtain drawn back to indicate a new scene, Grace's demeanor completely changed. Gone was the brisk if slightly anxious professional, and in her place was the tremulous love and pride of a mother watching her son find his wings.

"I've never seen anything like it," she said. "He was like a different boy as soon as he had it in his hands. As long as he had it pointed at something, he could talk to me like he's trusted me his whole life."

John had often wondered over the years if his little brother would have had the same affinity for photography as he did or if he'd ever been given the chance to find out. That question may never get answered for him, but hearing that Toby, a little boy who reminded him so much of his memories of Simon, did seem to have that connection sent a wave of emotion through him. It made him more determined than ever to protect Toby and his guardian.

"I would love to teach him," he offered. "It sounds like he's a natural."

"I'm sure he would like that," Grace said. "He keeps asking about you."

"He does?" John struggled for what else to say. He was well aware of the difficulty Grace was having in feeling accepted by Toby. He was uneasy when he couldn't read the emotion behind what she had told him.

"Well, it's a nice thought," Grace said, the briskness back. She heaved a breath and straightened her shoulders as if preparing herself for something. "Since I've given you a clean bill of health, I'm sure you'll be on your way as soon as possible."

She opened the door, indicating that their time was over, but instead of exiting, John stayed where he was.

He silently said the closest thing to a prayer that he could remember offering in a long time.

Am I doing the right thing?

No warning voice came to stop him, so he looked Grace in the eye and said, "Actually, I think I am going to be staying for a while."

Grace was making homemade pizza for supper that night, and kneading the dough gave her an opportunity to try to untangle her thoughts. She'd been struggling to do that ever since John announced his intentions to stay in Living Skies, at least for the time being.

But how long was that going to be? She couldn't imagine it would take long for him to teach Toby everything he would be able to handle at his age. Toby might have formed a quick attachment to his camera, but he was only five years old.

Besides, he was already forming an attachment to John. Being as objective as she could manage, without letting pangs of envy get in the way, Grace had to consider what it would do to the little boy to become even more attached and then have John leave. Because no matter what John was saying right now, she couldn't believe his intention to stay would last long.

That had something to do with his father, but that subject was off-limits for John and her.

The farther away they steered from a conversation that might reveal her alcoholism, the better.

As she kneaded the dough, Toby snapped pictures of the awaiting ingredients on the counter, giving a running commentary as he did so.

"These are toe-may-toes. They are red and squishy. This is orange cheese, and this is..." he hesitated and looked up at Grace "...butter?"

"It's a different kind of cheese," Grace explained, her heart expanding at the easy way he was interacting with her. "It's called mozzarella, and it gets all melty and makes the pizza really delicious. It gets really stretchy too. I'll show you after the pizza bakes."

"Mot-za-rella," Toby repeated and took pictures of it from two different angles. "Somethin' green," he continued. "I won't be eating *that*."

Grace muffled a giggle. She was enjoying his chatter so much and didn't want to embarrass him.

She didn't believe what Child's Garden Daycare said about him. She knew all too well that

Toby had more triggers than any child his age should have, but that wasn't his fault. Why couldn't they see that inside was a sweet, intelligent boy with the potential to grow up into a fine young man?

As if in response to her thoughts, Grace's phone trilled with the sound that signaled she had an email. The preview window told her that it was from one of the daycares she had contacted.

Her heart drummed a beat of nervous anticipation. Worried the email would be another no and she would have to carry that into supper, she decided she would look at it later. She didn't want anything to ruin what she and Toby had going here.

"Grace?"

He so rarely addressed her directly. Grace put her phone on the counter face down and out of reach and turned to him.

He snapped a picture of her.

"Hey, I wasn't ready," she teased. She ran her fingers exaggeratedly through her hair and struck some silly model poses. Toby's laugh rang out, and it was like unwrapping a long-awaited gift.

At supper, though, her thoughts kept wandering to the unread email, as well as to John's offer to teach Toby about taking pictures. While

Toby pulled two slices of pizza apart, eyeing the cheese that was as stretchy as she had promised, Grace made the decision that she could at least face the answer to one of those quandaries.

"I'll be right back," she told Toby and went to get her phone. She added gently, "You should have a bite of that pizza."

Toby's hands froze, and for a moment, she was afraid that she had shattered the ease of the evening, but then he took a bite and chewed thoroughly.

Grace let out the breath she'd been holding. She knew that she had to stop being afraid. Toby needed love, and part of love was consistent and reasonable guidelines.

She returned to the table and clicked open the email message.

Thank you for your application to place your child, Toby, in our daycare facility. Although Toby sounds like a fine young boy, we regret to inform you...

Not wanting Toby to notice that she was upset, Grace stifled a sigh, picked up a slice of pizza and took a large bite. She would read the email more carefully later, on the off chance they had left even the tiniest door cracked open, but she wasn't holding out much hope.

Frankly, the whole thing had the ring of a form letter with the child's name inserted into the appropriate parts. Her teeth tore off her next bite rather ferociously.

"When am I going back to school?" Toby asked.

Grace swallowed with some difficulty. He had a way of doing that, of zeroing in on the very thing that she was trying to keep from him. In this case, it was to protect him from worry, but she was all too aware that his young life had been filled with unhealthy secrets, so she decided to answer him.

"You'll go back as soon as I find a better school for you."

"But I liked that school," Toby said, his eyes wide with quizzical innocence. "The teachers were nice."

Grace's eyes welled up with tears, which she rapidly blinked away. She grabbed a tissue and pretended to sneeze into it.

There was no way in the world she was telling him that the teachers had a problem with him. It was clear that he had no perception of how his outbursts impacted people. He seemed hardly aware that they happened. Grace was sure there was no malice in them.

This was a moment that might have had her reaching for the solace of an ice-cold beer at one time. Instead, she prayed silently but intensely. She knew enough not to push herself to the edge of temptation and would call her sponsor if she needed to.

In the meantime, though, there was a little boy wearing a goatee of pizza sauce who was intuitive enough to wonder why he wasn't in school. What was she going to tell him? How would she fill his days?

John.

The pros and cons danced, stepping on each other's toes, while she washed the dishes. Toby continued his picture-snapping spree instead of drying them for her. He was happy, and she needed the time to think.

John's repeated offer to help was, of course, first and foremost in her mind. It occurred to her that if she could get Toby focused on that, she could buy herself a short reprieve from having to come up with some kind of palatable explanation about why he wasn't welcome at his daycare anymore. And why it might be difficult to find a welcome at another one.

No, there were no words. Her hands clenched under the soapy water. Toby had been dealt an unfair hand in life, and while she believed that the Lord could patch up the biggest holes, that didn't mean there wasn't very real and very human pain while the wounds gaped open.

When Grace was tucking Toby into bed that night and listening to his prayers, she made her decision.

After they said amen together, she said, "Toby, you remember John?"

He nodded and pulled the covers up under his nose, his eyes wide.

"He wants to teach you how to take pictures. Would you like that?"

He nodded vigorously without hesitation. It was worth everything to see the way his face lit up with utter joy.

"When?" he asked eagerly. "Tomorrow?"

"I'll have to see when John is free," Grace said. Her heart skipped a beat at the thought of calling him and giving him the news, which was completely ridiculous. This was about giving Toby a boost through a rough time. It wasn't about her at all.

Or about a rugged man with the gentlest eyes she'd ever seen.

She smoothed the covers under Toby's chin. Instead of a good-night kiss, which she knew he would shy away from, she softly touched his nose with one finger.

"Sleep tight," she said. "I'm here if you need anything."

Just as Grace was in the process of slowly easing Toby's door partway shut, leaving enough space for the hallway light to filter in, his drowsy voice reached her.

"You'll come take pictures too, right?"

He wants me.

"Yes… Yes, I can do that." The important thing was that he wanted her to come with him, and she'd said yes. She would figure out the details later.

But the problem of taking time away from work continued to plague Grace long into the evening, distracting her from the devotional book based on the Psalms that she was trying to read.

She had never been able to understand why some people considered Psalms an easy book of the Bible. Granted, it wasn't filled with hard-to-pronounce names and convoluted lineages, but it cut so deeply to the core of all human emotion that she sometimes felt like there was a spotlight on her, exposing all of her secrets while she read it.

Tonight, though, the words on the page just couldn't compete with her racing thoughts.

The problem was that she had been so eager for Toby's happiness and acceptance that she had made him promises before she'd taken time to really think through how it was all going to work—or if it would work at all.

Of course, she had always known that she

wasn't just going to send Toby off with John by himself, no matter how trustworthy a vibe she got from him. He kind of reminded her of a grizzly bear that would do anything to protect Toby. She'd thought she could figure something out with Carol Barker or maybe with Vivian Russell. She could ask one of them if they'd mind tagging along on a picture-taking spree.

Why hadn't it even occurred to her that she could be the one going along? Was it because she hadn't expected Toby to want her or because she didn't want to allow herself to get her hopes up? Or was it because she thought staying away from John would be the kindest thing to do for her heart?

But this was all for Toby. Someway, she would make it work: She would reschedule appointments. She would take a long-overdue vacation. If Toby wanted her to be there, she would do whatever it took to make that happen.

With that goal firmly in mind, she phoned John.

"Hello?" He sounded out of breath.

"John? It's Grace. Did I catch you at a bad time? You're not overdoing it on your ankle, are you?"

"No, all good. You just caught me in the middle of some sit-ups. A guy could go a bit stir-crazy here."

Sit-ups.

A picture of John Bishop working out flashed through her mind, and she found it all too appealing.

Sternly reminding herself of her purpose in calling, Grace grabbed the anchor he had unwittingly given. "Did you mean what you said about helping Toby learn about taking pictures?" Then she added in a rush, like it was a confession she had to get out, "He wants me to join you too."

She clamped her jaw tight, stopping herself from asking if that was okay with him. She wasn't a girl in high school who needed a boy's approval. She had never been someone who was tempted by popularity or by getting attention. Her temptation was in a bottle, and the Lord was helping her deal with that one day at a time.

Although it was over the phone, she could almost feel John go still, thinking.

Or maybe she was reading too much into it; maybe he was just catching his breath.

She really had to stop thinking about him working out.

"Of course I meant what I said," John answered. "When you get to know me, you'll learn that I never say things that I don't mean."

The words hung between them like a promise Grace doubted he'd meant to give.

She didn't really expect that she'd be getting to know him, not in any depth at least. Because as much as he saw something in Toby and wanted to help him, she still believed that his real goal was to get out of Living Skies as quickly as he could.

Chapter Seven

He was a man who had no interest whatsoever in a serious relationship. He'd adopted a nomadic lifestyle in part to avoid that very thing, and he would be long gone from Living Skies again if it wasn't for a certain little boy who tugged at his heart. There was absolutely no rhyme or reason for the way his heart skipped a beat when that little boy's foster mother said she would be joining them on their picture-taking excursions.

Excursions? Plural?

John studied the face in the mirror. He'd never brag about it. In fact, he was decidedly uncomfortable with it. More than one woman had let him know that they found him attractive, but all he saw was someone who had experienced some things at too early an age. It all showed in his eyes. He also needed a shave. Well, he couldn't do anything about the first, but he picked up his razor and began to work on the second.

For him, shaving was a kind of meditation. It always relaxed him and gave him a few quiet minutes to think things through. Often, he used the time to visualize his next photo shoot. How he would utilize the light to capture the flicker of pure honesty when someone let their mask down for a fleeting moment.

But right now, he was using the time to try to discipline himself not to make the situation more than it was. There was no way it would take him more than a morning or afternoon—a couple of hours really—to teach Toby the things about photography that he could manage at his age.

So why was he imagining the outings that the three of them could have together? The more places he went to in Living Skies, the more risk there was of running into his father, but even that didn't stop his imagination from running on.

Well, he told himself, if they kept seeing him, eventually his father would let his own mask slip—he had never been able to keep it in place for long—and Grace would see for herself.

John scraped off the remaining patch of bristle and patted on some spicy aftershave. He couldn't help wondering what Grace's reaction would be when she saw him.

Maybe he would ask her how she had gotten to know his father and why she trusted him. It would help to know what he was working with.

John quickly made the bed and tidied up. One thing was for sure, even if he was going to stay for just a little while longer, he had to find somewhere else to call his temporary home. Small, stifling motel rooms were not exactly his style. If there had been a place to pitch a tent, he would have chosen that instead.

Of course, he hadn't thought he would still be here.

His ankle had improved in a shorter time than he—or his pretty PT—had anticipated, but it still cried out for relief at times. John sank onto the bed, knocking the Bible that the motel had provided for the room onto the carpet.

He leaned over, picked it up and sat holding it thoughtfully for a moment.

He had started reading bits of it early in the morning, or at night when he couldn't sleep. Mostly it had been as a way to alleviate boredom. He still didn't think he was ready to make a full commitment to God anytime soon. He had a lot of explaining to do about parents who were allowed to run away from their children when the going got tough.

Still, there was something about the stark honesty of the words in the way the Bible dealt as openly about sorrows as it did about joys and accomplishments. He was starting to think there must be something—he wasn't quite sure what yet, but *something*—to it. Something he hadn't been willing to consider for a long time.

What if I tried praying?

The thought nudged him, and he was nervous but intrigued, like he was sitting in front of a buffet of delectable dishes that he had never tried, that were definitely unknown to him, but he had the sense that they might offer more sustenance than any he'd ever known.

God—he ventured cautiously—*I need a place to live if there's anything You can do about that. Oh, that is, if I'm meant to stay here.*

He sighed and lightly raked his fingernails down the side of his freshly shaven cheek. He'd probably done it all wrong, but you couldn't blame a guy for trying.

He had a quick stop to make at *The Chronicle* before meeting up with Grace and Toby at her place. Grace had said that she might as well drive, because it was easier than giving him directions for the place she had in mind. He was the photographer and had a knack for maneuvering his way around much more complicated terrain than the Saskatchewan prairies, but he didn't argue.

It was enough that he was spending time in her company—*For the purpose of giving Toby some photography tips*, he hastily reminded himself.

John pulled up in front of *The Chronicle*'s office and parked the car. He hadn't questioned Vivian's request that he meet her here on a Saturday. The paper had always kept its own hours depending on what was going on. Stew was as likely to spontaneously give everyone a day off as to call them in at a moment's notice.

He assumed that Vivian, being a representative of Stew's persistence, once again intended to pitch him the job. Well, this time, he would surprise her. He would say that he was willing to stay for as long as it took to find a permanent editor.

But when he saw Vivian, the anxious creases in her face didn't spell business.

"I'm sorry to drag you down here," Vivian jumped in without preamble. "But Bill's packing at the house, and he's fit to be tied, so I figured it would be easier to talk to you here. I tell you, that man of mine doesn't lose his cool very often, but when he does, you don't want to be around him, which is partly why I'm hiding out here."

John's brain scrambled to play catch-up. He was usually adept at pulling pieces together to make a whole story, but this one had him lost.

"Vivian… Vivian," he finally interjected when she was about to launch into a discussion of rolling versus folding clothes in order to save room in a suitcase. "What's going on? Why am I here?"

"Oh, didn't I say that part?" She looked genuinely surprised, leaving John to wonder even more what had befallen *The Chronicle*'s usually unflappable receptionist and all-around office guru.

"No, you did not."

"Well—" her mouth trembled and then thinned into a firm line "—it seems that our Charlie has decided that he is quitting university. He called last night to tell us that instead of going back for the fall semester, he's going to be traveling with his buddies, working where he can and seeing where the road takes them."

Vivian sounded dismayed but it didn't sound all that bad to John. Of course, he was used to a nomadic lifestyle—that *was* his life—but from some conversations with Vivian, he knew that the Russells were proud of Charlie being premed.

"So, you're going there to try to talk some sense into him?" he ventured a guess.

"Yes," Vivian said with grim determination. "Some things just have to be dealt with in person."

John was still wondering what his role was in all of this. He listened to Vivian extol the virtues of straightforward communication for a few minutes before he took his own straight-forward approach.

"Ah, Vivian, I'm supposed to be meeting Grace, so…"

For a moment, Vivian seemed to forget her own concerns, and her eyes snapped with interest.

"Meeting Grace?"

He grimaced inwardly at the unwanted focus.

"I'm teaching her foster son a little bit about photography," he said, and hoped she would leave it at that. But they really had to get to the point of this visit.

"Vivian, if you need me to keep an eye on the paper while you're gone, just say so. I'll do what I can."

"The paper?" Vivian blinked at him. "Oh, yes, sure. That would be great, but that's not what I wanted to talk to you about. I wondered if you would mind staying at our house while we're gone. Once Bill and I got to talking about it, we realized we haven't taken a break for a while. Naturally, our first priority is to talk some sense into Charlie, but we thought since we're going anyway, we might as well carry on and make a bit of a holiday out of it. So we'd need you for about two weeks, if you wouldn't mind."

"I wouldn't mind," John answered, process-ing it all. "I wouldn't mind at all. It would be my pleasure."

"Well, that's settled, then." Vivian clapped her hands together and spun to get her beast of a purse off her desk. Every time John saw it, he expected her to pull a Mary Poppins and retrieve anything from a lamp to a beach umbrella from its depths.

She rummaged and came up with a set of keys. "Come over later for a quick walk-through. How does seven sound?"

He nodded and took the keys.

"Bring Grace with you, if you like," she said with what he could've sworn was a simper. "You can both stay for tea."

"Oh, I'm sure you must have a lot of packing to do," John said. Good manners as well as a sudden throbbing in his ankle kept him from bolting out the door. But he did make his excuses as soon as he could.

It wasn't until he was in his car headed toward Grace's house that he remembered his somewhat lackadaisical prayer. He had asked for a different place to live…

No, it couldn't be.

It was only house-sitting, he told himself. It wasn't a permanent home, and it definitely couldn't be an answer to a prayer.

Still, it was enough to make a man pause and think.

Grace and Toby came out the front door as

soon as John pulled up, like they'd been waiting for him. They smiled like he was the person they most wanted to see, and it made him take another pause and think about what it would be like to stay in one place, to settle down, to have someone there waiting for him…

He mentally shook his head. Even if that ever happened, which was unlikely, he would never settle in Living Skies, not with his father here.

"Do you want the front seat?" he asked Toby and noticed a flicker of surprise and something else in Grace's eyes.

What, did she think he was going to pull rank just because he was bigger and older? This outing was for Toby.

The boy himself was almost trembling with the kind of nervous excitement that John recognized when good things happened to someone who had learned not to expect them—perhaps not to trust them either.

He reached up and took the camera he had hanging around his neck and gently placed it around Toby. It set the boy slightly off balance for a second or two, but he clutched the camera with both hands, lifting it up so that it didn't dangle down so low on him. He looked up at John, his eyes a bright question mark.

"I promise to teach you how to use your own camera," John told him, "but this one is mine, and it takes great pictures. I want you to give it a try too, because the more you know about different cameras, the better a photographer you'll be. And I want you to know that I only let really good friends use my camera, okay, bud?"

Toby nodded vigorously and smiled a wide, gap-toothed smile that John hadn't known the boy was capable of.

Grace caught his eye and mouthed a thank-you at him.

Suddenly, he was sure this was going to be a very good day.

Grace carefully maneuvered her vehicle onto a dirt road approximately twenty minutes outside of Living Skies' town boundaries and drew to a stop.

Conversation during the drive had gone easily, with Toby calling out questions about the camera from the back seat and she and John bickering comfortably over what to listen to on the radio.

A little too comfortably?

"I can't believe you're a seventies rock fan," John said, shaking his head slowly in mock dismay.

"I can't believe *you're* an eighties ballads fan," she retorted.

They ended up settling on a country music

station. Grace's fingers tapped out the beat on the steering wheel. John drummed out a matching beat, his fist against his thigh, and it suddenly felt all too coupley and family-like.

That was exactly what she was *not* looking for.

It was too risky to get close to people. Vulnerabilities were exposed, and secrets were revealed—secrets that were sure to chase people away, especially someone like John Bishop.

There was no telling how he would react if he ever found out that she shared the addiction he could not find it in himself to forgive his father for.

No, scratch that, she knew exactly how he would react.

Besides, she liked living life on her own terms, by her own schedule. If things went the way she wanted them to with the evening classes at the community center continuing to expand, and she got to help people discover ways to be healthy and lead fulfilling lives, she would have even less time to consider a relationship.

Not that anyone was asking her to be in one.

"Grace, are you okay?" John said.

"How come we aren't getting out of the car?" Toby piped up from the back seat.

She realized that she sat frozen, her hands still locked into position on the steering wheel.

"Was it the comments I made about the music you like?" John asked, and she could hear teasing in his voice even before she turned to see the droll twinkle in his eyes. "Because I swear, I don't judge you by it. You can even play some on the way home and try to win me over."

Try to win me over...

Was John Bishop flirting with her, or did she just want to think that?

The butterflies the thought gave her were nudged away by the comment about judging. Joking or not, he might not judge her by her musical tastes, but he would certainly judge her if he knew the secret she kept from almost everyone.

Toby stuck his head over the seat and looked back and forth between them.

"Let's go!" he said.

"Yes, absolutely." Grace tore her gaze from John's eyes. They held a question she wasn't at all ready to answer. She opened the car door and stepped out. The others followed suit.

There was a wide span of prairie land outside of the town limits that Grace considered to be absolutely beautiful. It was a quiet beauty, one you had to be patient and look for, and she was suddenly anxious that John, with all of his experience taking stunning photos in any number of striking and exotic locations, would find this location dull and uninspiring.

But when she tentatively looked at him to catch his reaction, the raw emotion she saw there ripped through her like a tidal wave.

"Hey, sorry." His eyes darted her way, and he knuckled quickly under them in a way that made Grace think for one dizzying moment that he was going to cry.

But he smiled instead and said, "Wow, memories. Are you sure that *you're* not a photographer?" he added, teasing now in a way that Grace found almost dangerously appealing. Or maybe she was just glad to see that he wasn't going to break down.

Keep telling yourself that.

"What do you mean?" she asked, matching his smile.

"I mean that this happens to be the exact spot that Stew sent me to when I wanted to start taking pictures for *The Chronicle*. He said that if I could find pictures here that caught people's attention, I'd know I was really onto something."

"Because at first glance, there doesn't seem to be much to look at," Grace concluded, marveling at the way his words sent her earlier concerns flying into the wind.

She was aware of that emotion warming her smile as she looked up at John. He looked down, and whatever he saw on her face caused his own smile to falter a bit. His eyes were quizzical, but then he beamed back at her in a way that made her think that...

Toby huffed out an impatient sigh, and the moment passed.

"Right with you, bud," John said, reaching out to ruffle the boy's hair.

Grace watched for Toby to pull away or at least flinch, but he only grinned. "I wanna take pictures."

"Me too," John said. "That's what we came here for."

Of course that was what they'd come for. She didn't know what had happened to her a few minutes back. Her chagrin over the way she had been on the edge of acting like a schoolgirl with a massive crush mingled in an unsettling way with envy. She knew that was wrong, but she still couldn't quite rid herself of feeling jealous over the way John was making strides with Toby that she was unable to.

She reminded herself once again that the important thing was that Toby did make strides. He needed to start to believe that people could be trusted. It shouldn't matter who the person was who made that happen, much as she wanted it to be her.

A little ways from her, she could see John

and Toby crouching. John gestured that Toby should part the grass and take a closer look. When Toby pointed at something and looked up with a question on his face, John smiled, nodded and showed him how to aim the camera at it.

It was great to see the two of them together, even if it made her throat thicken.

She lifted her chin. She wasn't an outsider. She *was* Toby's foster mother, a role she treasured, despite her concern that she wasn't doing as good a job at it as she wanted to. She was also a single, independent professional with her own goals.

The evening programs she was running were going fairly well, but there was always room for improvement. Although she did a few presentations herself, the main role she had taken on was to keep alert as to the kinds of topics people would be interested in and find the right ways and people to bring them that information.

John was pointing at something in a tree, and Grace followed Toby's intense gaze with her own until she spotted a black-capped chickadee blending into the branches of the tree.

Would others benefit by using photography as a way to get in touch with some emotions they might find difficult to deal with? Well, maybe that question wasn't even worth asking, since there was no reason to believe that John would be willing to teach it.

There was no reason to believe he would stick around at all.

Still, she thoughtfully pulled her phone out of her pocket, intending to make a record of the idea, then wished she had left her phone alone.

An email response from another daycare had come in earlier, but Grace had deliberately chosen not to bring stress into her morning or to ruin the anticipation of today by opening it.

She avoided asking herself why she assumed it would be bad news. Didn't her faith mean more to her than that?

She did believe in God, but maybe if she understood, even for herself, why she had taken to drinking the way she had, things would make more sense.

That was another reason why she was reluctant to tell many people about her addiction. Everyone was always looking for the big, elusive why, and she simply didn't have an answer to give them.

The unopened email was right there on her phone screen. Okay, no putting it off any longer. It wasn't like she was going to fall to pieces when she got the answer, especially not in front of John.

Toby was happily preoccupied, avidly watching gopher holes for one of their occupants to make an appearance, camera at the ready. She saw how eagerly he was already mimicking John's stance and gestures, and she breathed out a prayer, not only for the answer that the email held, but for the hope that she could be a positive role model in Toby's life.

As she scanned the first few lines of the email, Grace let out the breath she'd been holding. They wanted to meet with her and Toby. They weren't prepared to make any promises, not even after the meeting, but at least they weren't already saying no.

Grace's knees buckled slightly. The relief slamming into her was somehow more powerful than disappointment would have been. She hid her face in her hands for a moment, and her prayer of thanks carried a sprinkling of guilt that she didn't have more trust.

She tucked the phone back into her pocket and looked up to see John striding toward her with Toby trotting behind him.

"What's wrong?" John and Grace asked each other.

Toby raised his camera and made a record of their mutually confused looks.

"Nothing's wrong here," John said. "I came over to see what was wrong with you. I saw you look at your phone, and then you put your head in your hands. Bad news?"

He saw that? The man really did have an eye for detail.

"Actually, it's good news," she said. "A day-care wants Toby and me to come in for an interview. It's not a definite yes, but at least they didn't say no. I guess the relief just hit me."

"That's good, then," John said. "That's great news."

"Thanks for checking on me," Grace said after a moment.

She wasn't quite sure how the grumpy, unco-operative patient in her office had changed into this man who noticed what was going on with her and appeared to genuinely care. All she did know was she couldn't let herself begin to count on that. What's more, she didn't want to.

The only problem was that it was getting harder to convince herself of that.

Chapter Eight

Sitting at Bill and Vivian Russell's kitchen table, John took in his surroundings and again pondered the prompt answer he had received to his prayer. He wondered if Grace had been praying about Toby's daycare situation. She likely was. He added his own prayer for the success of the meeting she and Toby were attending this afternoon.

It was getting easier to let his thoughts turn into prayers, though he still wasn't sure exactly what faith was going to mean in his life.

He suspected Vivian felt a little guilty leaving *The Chronicle*'s office in his hands, along with looking after her house, but he reassured her it was fine.

He'd gotten used to the idea of being back at the paper. It was also solace for him. The smell. The sense of stories swirling around in the air almost as if they existed and had a life of their own before anyone tamed them enough to commit them to print. The nearness of coffee and store-bought cookies, which were never the best but were so much part of the whole experience. He would enjoy it all.

In a small town like Living Skies, the paper had never required much staff. There was an editor to keep things organized and to write articles. Vivian kept the office organized and running smoothly in her inimitable way. Stew, of course, was still the guardian from afar. John believed it would stay that way until Stew's dying day. There were also the occasional freelancers that contributed articles, but the news always seemed to mostly take care of itself.

"There are always a few recipes you could run if you need to fill up space," Vivian told him before her departure. "But I'm not expecting you to feel obligated. The paper has gone on hiatus before. When the last editor was let go, we took a break, and we survived. Maybe it's a good thing we don't live in the news capital of the world."

After Vivian and her husband left, John sat reminiscing about how this office and Stew had turned him from a frightened, defeated young man into someone who believed he might have a shot at making something of his life. He knew there was no way he could refuse to help the newspaper, at least to get on solid ground again.

Funny, though, how the first person he wanted to let know about his decision wasn't Stew Wagner. He wanted to call Grace. But he did call Stew first and give a verbal commitment before he could talk himself out of it.

He was glad, though, that he and Grace and Toby—who was the important one here—had plans to meet up after supper to look through the photographs that he'd helped the little boy take. He was anxious to hear how the meeting with the daycare facility went.

Vivian had told him to make their home his home, indicating that he should feel free to play host there. But he wasn't quite comfortable with that. Maybe he would offer to treat Grace and Toby to pie at Murphy's and take his chances on running into his father.

My father...

Somehow, he'd managed to forget about him for a few minutes while caught up in the emotion of giving back.

Well, he had made his promise to Stew, and he wasn't going back on it. He was also a grown man, not a scared little boy anymore, and he would face his father whenever and however he had to.

He would do it for the sake of the newspaper that had shown him that life hadn't slammed the door all the way shut on him.

And for the little boy who reminded him of his brother and for that boy's lovely foster mother.

John checked his watch. It wouldn't be long before Grace and Toby went to the interview. He again asked the God he was trying to get reacquainted with to help them get the answer they needed.

In the meantime, he had to think about what kind of cover story would get the paper going at full force again. He found some back issues and started flipping through them, pausing to make notes.

He noticed that a popular feature—one that garnered many responses—was a column called Grateful. The author, whoever he or she was, simply signed the column that same way.

John was struck by the fact that it wasn't an overly saccharine, Pollyanna way of listing happy things at the expense of ignoring the reality of life. No, this author understood that finding happiness in life was hard-earned, and that made those good moments, when they came, all the sweeter.

John thought suddenly of the warm, clean scent of Grace when she leaned in close to check his ankle. He thought of the joy that flitted across her face whenever she connected with Toby and the way her hair looked beautiful in the simple style she wore... Gratitude was like a fragile bird coming to light on his shoulder.

The interview at the daycare had gone well enough to give Grace a buoying kind of hope.

In answer to her prayers, Toby had actually done remarkably well. Of course, even though he wasn't with them, she had to give John most of the credit for that. Toby had been so content to talk about the man and the pictures they had taken together. He'd said he couldn't wait to look through them with John, and it had hardly registered with him where they were going and what they were doing.

John had insisted that Toby could take John's camera with him, and he wore it around his neck like a security blanket. Throughout the interview, he'd been a little boy who couldn't sit still, but he'd also been a little boy who clearly had the potential to show great interest in learning about something.

"As I said, we can't make any promises," Ms. Kaiswatum, the kind-eyed director of the Adventures in Learning Daycare, said. "I have to talk this over with my peers, but I will say that I really enjoyed meeting you and Toby today. I do plan to make a recommendation that we find space for him." She stood up and extended her hand.

"Thank you, Ms. Kaiswatum," Grace said, also standing and extending her own hand. "You have no idea how much this means to me."

"Call me Ruby," the director said. They both looked at Toby, who was aiming John's camera at a container of pens and pencils on her desk.

The director smiled. "I think I have some idea what it means," she said.

Now, driving home, Grace sang one of her favorite songs of praise.

"You don't sing that good," Toby remarked after a few bars of it.

She burst out laughing. "You've got that right," she said, thinking how wonderfully strange it was that someone could feel so happy after being insulted.

If Toby was accepted into the daycare, there would definitely be some things to work out. The commute would be about forty minutes, and she didn't want to have to rely on others to take Toby to and fro, so it would mean adjusting her work schedule. She could do it and she absolutely *would* do it because anything was worth getting Toby into a place where he felt safe and welcome. A place that would help him grow to his full potential.

The way John also seemed eager to help him.

She still hadn't quite figured out why she trusted the man the way she did. She'd only known him a few weeks. She figured that much of it had to do with the way Toby so readily trusted him. But what made him want to reach out to Toby? She knew little about John's past, other than he was estranged from his father. She couldn't imagine what a decent Christian man had done that was so unforgiveable. Maybe Toby reminded him of a son… She had no way of knowing what he'd done in the past or who he'd run away from, other than his father.

That thought sat uneasily, tripping across her stomach like it was on a rocking boat trying to get its sea legs. That wasn't John's style, not at all. He might not want to settle in one place for long, but he would never run from his responsibilities. She didn't know how she was so sure of that, but she was.

Still, when they got together that evening, she planned to find out more about him.

In the rearview mirror, she could see Toby snapping pictures out the car window as the prairie slid by in a collage of wheat, flax and canola fields. Soon it would be time to harvest. In Saskatchewan, the crops signaled the passage of time as readily as any traditional holiday.

"Did you like Ms. Kaiswatum?" Grace asked, trying to catch Toby's eye in the mirror.

He nodded but then added, "When are we going to see John?"

"Tonight after supper," Grace said. "We're going to go to Murphy's. That'll be fun, right? Maybe you can get chocolate milk."

"And look at my pictures with John."

"Yes, and look at your pictures."

Toby sat back in his car seat with a contented sigh. "I took some great ones," he said.

Throughout their supper of beef stew that she had left simmering in the slow cooker all day, Grace argued with her nerves. It was ridiculous for her to be so on edge when meeting John at Murphy's was absolutely *not* a date.

She brushed out her hair so that it fell in soft waves to her shoulders and added a touch of mascara and lip gloss to her freshly washed face. She was going out in public, and despite favoring a natural look, it wasn't wrong to want to look her best.

Toby had dribbled gravy down the front of his shirt at supper, so she helped him change it and told him to go and brush his teeth and hair. Excited over their outing, he was quick to obey.

Not all that long ago, he would have been fearfully apologetic about the spilled gravy. When she sponged at the spot, he smelled of the grass in the field, and of earthy little boy, and he squirmed like any little boy would, but he wasn't afraid of her, and for that, she thanked God.

Murphy's was busy when they arrived. There

was rarely a time when it wasn't busy. Its welcoming atmosphere, comfortable decor and homemade meals made from the proprietor's grandmother's recipe collection all combined to ensure that it was a place people wanted to return to again and again.

As the savory smells of chicken pot pie, fresh salmon and hamburgers with onions coaxed to sweetness in a buttery pan tantalized her nose, Grace almost regretted eating supper at home.

But her stew had turned out well, if she did say so herself. More importantly, preparing meals for Toby and sitting down to eat with him was one of the best ways to show him that she was willing and happy to provide for him.

John was already at a table. He was making friendly conversation with Michelle, one of Grace's favorite servers. The young Indigenous girl was serious and hardworking. She was shy but friendly and she possessed a gentle sense of humor once she was comfortable. Knowing that Michelle's goal was to attend university to become a speech pathologist, Grace always made sure to leave a generous tip.

As she and Toby made their way toward the table, the little boy's steps bounced with excitement. She saw by the smile on Michelle's face that John had succeeded in making her comfortable.

He also looked relaxed in a way that Grace hadn't seen yet. It softened the rugged lines of his face and made him undeniably more attractive. His moss green shirt and freshly combed hair made her wonder if he had taken care with his own appearance, the way she was willing to admit—at least to herself—that she had done.

Michelle greeted them, exchanged a fist bump with Toby and then resumed her professional role, her pen and pad poised to take their order.

Toby wanted chocolate milk, and the adults ordered decaf coffee.

"Can I tempt you with pie?" Michelle offered. "Erin," she added, naming their baker extraordinaire, "made a lemon meringue today, and it's delicious."

"I'm sure it is," Grace said, "but I'm still full from supper." Still, she looked at John, almost hopeful that he would urge her to change her mind.

"I'll tell you what," John said, obviously picking up on her indecision, "bring us a piece and three forks. I'm sure we can all manage a bite or two."

"You won't regret it," Michelle promised. "I'll be right back with your coffees and the chocolate milk."

"You look nice," John said to Grace. "I mean, not that you don't always but... You know what

I mean." He chuckled as if embarrassed by his own compliment, ducking his head in a way that made Grace suddenly envision what kind of a boy he must have been.

It was disorienting to feel that he would have reminded her of Toby, and she briefly tried to imagine George Bishop as being anything other than the kind, Christian man she knew him to be.

But that wasn't something she wanted to think about, at least not yet.

"You look nice too," she said to John and then wondered if any two strong, responsible adults had ever blushed quite so much.

Michelle delivered their beverages, a slice of pie that wafted the scent of lemony goodness, and the requested three forks.

"Enjoy," she said.

Toby stuck his straw into his milk and blew bubbles until Grace gently put a stop to it. They all had a taste of the pie and found that it more than measured up to the rave review that Michele had given it.

After Toby swallowed his second bite, he said, "When are we gonna talk about my pictures?"

Grace's throat thickened slightly as she swallowed the taste of guilt along with the sweetness of the pie.

She hadn't exactly forgotten that the reason they were meeting in the first place was to go through the photos that John and Toby had taken, but she had allowed it to take second place to enjoying the sensation of being out with an attractive man who seemed to find her attractive too.

What is wrong with me?

John could almost physically sense Grace's emotional withdrawal. Suddenly, she was businesslike with him again, focusing her attention on Toby and his pictures.

Okay, two can play that game...

No, he mentally shook away that particular thought pattern. Grace wasn't playing a game with him, she was a dedicated foster mother and his probably soon-to-be-former PT. Well, who knew what she was to him now? He couldn't and wouldn't get into the habit of trying to analyze something that wasn't there.

Even if her hair looks especially soft tonight. Her lips especially glossy.

He flipped through the photographs, praising Toby for his efforts while giving him encouraging instruction about things he could try next time.

Michelle came along and offered more coffee, and to John's relief, Grace accepted a second cup. He was happy to see she wasn't eager to rush their evening to an end. He still had to tell her about his decision to stay in town for a while. For the sake of the newspaper, of course. At least, he would tell her that was the reason. He also wanted to know how their interview had gone at the daycare.

"I haven't even asked you how things went today," he said. "How was the interview?"

Before answering, Grace looked at Toby, who was neglecting his second glass of chocolate milk in favor of perusing the photographs again. He tilted his head and squinted at some, holding them almost up to his nose but careful not to touch his nose to them. He held the pictures by their edges the way John had taught him.

"It was good," she said. "So good, in fact, that I'm a little nervous at how hopeful I feel."

"It's good to have hope," John said and wondered if he was talking to himself as much as to her.

"When will you find out?" he asked.

"I don't know for sure, but I can't see it taking too long. Ms. Kaiswatum, the woman who interviewed us, more or less indicated that she thought Toby would fit in well there, but she has to talk it over with the rest of the staff. So maybe early next week."

"I don't mean to eavesdrop," Michelle, who had returned to their table to check on their coffee situation, said shyly. "Was your interview at Adventures in Learning?"

"Yes, that's right," Grace said. "Do you know the place?"

"Ms. Kaiswatum is my auntie Ruby," Michelle said with a smile. "I'll put in a good word for you. Not that I think you need one, but it can't hurt."

"No, it sure can't," Grace said.

She remained thoughtful for a moment after Michelle departed, and then she said, almost to herself, "Another God moment." She shook her head and glanced at John. "Not trying to get all preachy on you or anything."

It reminded John that he hadn't had a chance to share his own God experience with her. He wanted to tell her how his own prayer about a place to stay had been answered, and he now had another reason to stay.

He didn't know yet if Grace was also a reason to stay in town. At least, he wasn't ready to admit that to himself, but there was simply so much he wanted to share with her. He couldn't remember if he had ever experienced that feeling with another person.

Before he had discovered photography, he had kept his emotions locked up tightly in his heart. Sharing them had only made him a target.

Almost bashfully, he shared with Grace his

brief, almost throwaway prayer about a place to stay and the offer that had come from Vivian Russell shortly after.

Grace nodded. She seemed happy for him, but also like Vivian's offer was a perfectly natural thing.

"But after they're back from visiting their son and the rest of their vacation," he said, "I will be looking again, probably for an apartment to rent."

Grace tilted her head with a slow-building smile.

"Yup, I've decided to run *The Chronicle* for a while, at least until it has several good issues under its belt again and people know they can count on it after the fiasco with the previous editor."

"That's so great!" Grace exclaimed with enough enthusiasm in her tone to draw Toby's attention away from his pictures.

"What's so great?" he asked.

Grace raised her eyebrows at John, and he nodded that it was okay to tell Toby.

"Mr. Bishop is going to be staying here in Living Skies for a while longer," she said. "Isn't that nice? You'll be able to take more pictures with him."

Toby's exultant "Woo-hoo!" as he threw his hands up over his head partially helped erase the chagrined expression from Grace's face.

"It's okay for Toby to call me John," he said hurriedly, thinking about how much he disliked a name that made him think of his father.

"I'm booking up your time without even asking," Grace said.

"No, it's fine, honestly. I'm happy to do it."

A determined gleam came into her eyes, and she leaned forward in her chair. Again, he caught a whiff of her clean skin and a lingering hint of lemon on her breath. He disciplined himself not to close his eyes and inhale…

"How would you feel about teaching photography to more people?" she asked.

"Depends…" he said cautiously. "What did you have in mind?"

Grace told him about the evening program she coordinated and how she was always looking for interesting things to share with the participants.

"I think they would love you," she said.

"Can I give it some thought and get back to you?" he asked.

Her smile deflated slightly, but she said with determined cheerfulness, "Sure, that would be fine."

It wasn't that he didn't want to help, and teaching photography did sound like fun, but he was going to be busy with the paper, and he wasn't sure who would show up for the classes.

He wanted to ask Grace if his father was

likely to show up, but then again, he didn't want to know the answer to that.

Toby's eyes were starting to water from the yawns he suppressed, and John knew their evening was drawing to a close. He didn't want it to. At the very least, he wanted to know they were going to part with plans to see each other again, even if he hadn't been able to give Grace the answer she wanted.

"Are you busy tomorrow?" he asked.

This time, it was Grace's turn to look cautious. "I don't think so. I mean, the usual Saturday errands and whatnot. What did you have in mind?"

"I thought Toby might find it interesting to see how things come together at the newspaper." No, if he was doing this, if he was going to accept that he and Grace might have an actual friendship, he was going to start being more straightforward about it.

"You might find it interesting too," he amended. "And I'd really love to show you what I'll be doing there."

Chapter Nine

As Grace had hoped, she didn't have to wait long for the answer she had prayed for.

Ruby Kaiswatum phoned bright and early on Monday morning. "We would love to have Toby join us here at Adventures in Learning," she said. "I agree with you that he's a sweet boy with so much potential."

"Thank you. Thank you so much," Grace said fervently into the phone as she breathed the same gratitude toward Heaven. "When can he start?"

"Well, you will have to come in and sign some papers. I know you're a single mother with a full-time practice. Is it going to be difficult for you to figure out your schedule?"

"I'm sure I will be able to arrange things so that I'm not late picking Toby up," Grace said hurriedly.

In her head, she was rapidly calculating the cost of returned favors, excessively early mornings and perhaps catching up on paperwork in the evening. But she would figure it all out. She *had* to. The main thing was that Toby had a safe place to be during the day, a place that she trusted would help him reach his full potential.

"I am so grateful that you're taking a chance on Toby, Ms. Kaiswatum," she said. "By the way, I've discovered that I know your niece Michelle. She's a lovely girl."

"She has nothing but good things to say about you," the director said warmly. "And as I said before, please call me Ruby."

Today, Toby was spending the day with a family from church who had two rambunctious sons of their own. There was still a bit of time before Grace had to wake him up. She planned to drop him off at about ten to nine, just before her office opened. So Grace poured herself a cup of coffee and picked up the devotional on Psalms from the kitchen table. She flipped through the pages to find the day's reading, but her thoughts continued to distract her, scampering like squirrels every which way. She tried to turn them into nuggets of prayers that God could actually answer.

She hoped that Toby would see the news as a good thing. He hadn't said much about his experience at Child's Garden, but it made every muscle in her go tense when she thought about the staff making their doubts about Toby visible to him.

John would be happy to hear the news. Of course, now they would have less reason to see him.

She shook her head, slightly dismayed at herself for the direction of her thoughts, and tried to refocus on the daily reading.

Her phone rang again, and Grace frowned slightly. It appeared that between her disruptive thoughts and outside forces, a successful quiet time was not meant to be.

She thought about letting her voice mail pick up the call. She had to wake Toby up momentarily, if the phone hadn't done so already. But then she recognized the number and knew she had to take the call. It was Blanche Collins, Toby's caseworker.

"Hope I caught you at home," Blanche said in her no-nonsense way. Blanche was just edging toward middle age with lightly graying hair blunted off at the shoulders and pale blue eyes that had a way of studying people until the truth came out.

Grace knew that Blanche cared about Toby and always had the best interests at heart of all the children she worked with, which sometimes meant that she had to have a hard shell and make extremely tough decisions. It was easy to imagine that a soft, emotional person was hidden inside of Blanche's businesslike core, but Grace understood why she kept that person hidden and protected. Honestly, she knew she would never be able to do Blanche's job.

"I was just about to get Toby up," Grace said. "I'm dropping him off at a good family from our church to spend the day, but those arrangements are going to change soon."

She had kept Blanche appraised of the daycare situation and was happy to be able to tell her now that he had been accepted into a reputable daycare.

"I know that place," Blanche said. "It's a good one, and Ruby Kaiswatum and her staff are truly wonderful with those children. I'm glad it worked out. I actually called for a different reason," Blanche continued.

It didn't surprise Grace when Blanche made impromptu check-ins either by phone or in person. That was part of her job.

Grace tried to tell herself that it was her imagination that she heard caution in Blanche's voice, but a prickle of apprehension crawled up her spine nonetheless. She just hoped that this call ended on a good note.

"Now, I want you to remember that this is potentially good news," Blanche said. "It's what we ultimately strive for."

"I'm listening," Grace said, closing her eyes. In the background, she could hear Toby stirring, murmuring softly to himself.

It occurred to her that he hadn't cried out in his sleep since the night that John had happened by and his interest in taking photographs was sparked.

She forced herself to concentrate on what Blanche was telling her.

"Tiffany Bower has really been working her programs," Blanche said. "She's doing better than any of us anticipated or hoped for. She is attending meetings on a regular basis, and she has started attending a local church. She has even been asking for extra reading material and expressed an interest in taking classes on nutrition. She seems to grasp that her depression is something tangible that she can and should seek ongoing treatment for."

"Are you sure…it's for real?" Grace almost hated herself for asking, but she suddenly had a bit more empathy for why John couldn't simply accept the fact that his father had changed.

"Well, none of us are mind readers," Blanche said. "You can be sure I'll be monitoring things very closely. But as it stands now, I think I will be recommending that Tiffany be declared fit to parent again. I wanted you to know that."

Once again, Grace sensed that the caseworker

knew exactly how mixed Grace's feelings would be on the matter.

"As you said, it's what we all hope for," she somehow managed to say.

She was a sailboat when the wind had died and the words rested on her tongue, tasting like a lie.

"It won't be happening anytime too soon," Blanche said, as if that were a comfort. "But I thought the sooner I let you know, the sooner you can start making the adjustment."

So, she was at least acknowledging that it *would* be an adjustment.

Grace thanked her and was hanging up the phone just as Toby came into the room. He knuckled sleep out of his eyes, his pajama bottoms drooping in a way that made Grace want to hire a barrage of armored guards to protect him from everything always.

"Where am I goin' today?" he asked.

"To the Kardos'," Grace reminded him. "Get dressed, please, while I make your breakfast. We don't have long now before we have to leave."

Toby hesitated, and then to Grace's joyful astonishment, he voluntarily came over and leaned into her side for a moment.

She gently touched the top of his head and swallowed, thinking of the two phone calls she'd received that were going to change Toby's life.

One she trusted would be for good. The other she wasn't sure of at all.

Everything in her wanted to call John to hash over the phone calls she'd received that morning, especially the latter one, but that urge blindsided her even more.

The secret over her alcoholism aside, she had never been one who had to weigh out every decision, trivial or otherwise, with a gaggle of girlfriends or even her own parents. They'd always made it clear that they expected her to handle things and not be a bother to them.

So she could not understand why she was suddenly finding it difficult to get through her day, or even to sort out her own thoughts, without him.

What reason could John come up with to give Grace a call?

That was what he was pondering as he started a pot of coffee in the Russells' kitchen and slapped together a ham and cheese sandwich with mustard to take with him to the office.

He really shouldn't call her at all, not only because he knew she would be at work but because… Well, because he'd never needed someone to talk to, and he didn't want to start needing anyone now.

Still, he was genuinely interested in whether

Toby would be accepted into the daycare or not, and he was giving some serious consideration to Grace's request that he teach photography. But that would really mean putting down roots. Was he ready for that?

Will I ever be ready?

He had started walking to the office. It was good to strengthen his ankle, and despite his loner tendencies, he was experiencing a need to connect with this town where he had spent a brief but ultimately life-altering time. He wondered if he'd run into someone he remembered or if anyone would remember him.

Was it his feelings for Grace and his innate desire to protect Toby that had him thinking more about roots and connections? Was it his tentative, newly forming relationship with God?

Realizing that it would be nice to have a piece of fresh fruit to enjoy with his sandwich, John detoured into Graham's Grocers.

"Hi!" a pretty woman greeted him, her smile welcoming and her eyes filled with curiosity.

"I know you," she said, studying his face. Then she snapped her fingers, and her smile grew wide. "You're John Bishop, right?"

John nodded, unconsciously standing up straighter under the spotlight of recognition.

"You probably don't remember me," the woman said. "We didn't graduate together. I'm

Jenny Hart. It used to be Powell. I sure remember your yearbook pictures, and I know you're still into photography because I see your pictures everywhere. They are stunning."

"Thank you," John said, scratching his chin where his beard was already starting to grow back in, now self-conscious. His pictures were so much an extension of the things he struggled to express that he sometimes felt like he was being praised simply for having thoughts. Surely there were thousands upon thousands of people who deserved praise and recognition for the same thing.

But he smiled and thanked her.

"What can I help you with?" Jenny asked.

"I came in to get some fresh fruit to have with lunch," John explained.

"Hmm, I think apples are good right now." Jenny started to walk toward the produce section, and John followed.

She noticed his slight limp. "Are you all right?"

He nodded and briefly explained the fluke of an accident he'd had.

"Ooh, not good." Jenny wrinkled her nose and drew her shoulders forward in empathy.

"It's actually healed a lot faster than my physical therapist first expected. She's really great at what she does," he couldn't help adding. "You might know her. Grace Severight?"

It gave him a pleasant jolt to say her name out loud to someone.

"Yes, I know Grace." Jenny's eyes sparkled. "She is a great PT and a wonderful person. She kind of kept to herself in high school, if you know what I mean? But she's a good friend of mine, for sure."

John nodded. He did know. He certainly knew what it was like to keep to himself. He knew what his reasons had been, and now he couldn't help wondering what hers were.

"She's got a huge heart," Jenny continued. "I think she'd do anything to help someone."

To stop himself from battering this friendly woman with questions, John said, "So you recommend the apples?"

"The grapes are pretty good too." She pointed them out. "Do you prefer red or green?"

John chose an apple for his lunch, adding that he would be back later to stock up.

"I'm house-sitting for the Russells," he explained.

Jenny nodded as if that was a perfectly normal course of events. "Oh, yes, I hope they can convince their son to stay in school."

John experienced a strange but uncannily comforting sense of community. It was good to be seen, to be known. Maybe he could call Grace and tell her that he'd met a friend of hers. That would be good enough reason, wouldn't it?

Of course, he could simply phone her and ask if she had heard back from Adventures in Learning. Part of him wanted her to seek him out if she had good news to share. He wasn't sure why. He just knew that he wanted to be someone she turned to. And if Toby hadn't been accepted, he still wanted her to reach out.

In the meantime, there was work to be done at *The Chronicle*.

He turned on the computer, and as he waited for it to fire up, John's eyes were drawn to his own photographs displayed on the office walls. The town was proud to display the works of its successful son.

Anytime John saw his own work, it embarrassed him. He was always growing and learning new techniques. When he saw any previous work he'd done, even if it was from just a few months prior, it reminded him of a kid having their elementary school art up on a proud mother's refrigerator.

Not that he'd ever experienced that.

Studying them, he could mentally list the techniques he'd learned since then. When he took photos, his heart opened up, and he saw the world in a way he'd never dared to see it before, thus becoming a person he'd never dreamed he could be.

Surely trying to share that with people who might be struggling to find their own way was worth the risk of running into his father. Okay, he nodded with determination. He would do it.

There, now he had at least two solid reasons to call Grace. But he wouldn't interrupt her morning, and she wouldn't take a lunch break until at least twelve thirty, as she liked to go on the later side.

It was interesting, John mused, how he'd compiled these little details about her. The details weren't significant in themselves, but they all added up to the complex, wonderful and intriguing process of getting to know someone—really getting to know them.

He couldn't remember ever wanting to do that. He was always too busy protecting his heart and chronically preparing to leave rather than be left. But it was different with Grace. He couldn't pinpoint exactly why, except that he knew it wasn't just because of Toby anymore. Toby was important, and it mattered deeply to him that the boy have a happy, safe life and know he was loved and cared for.

But that wasn't everything he wanted. Not anymore.

There was no point in clock-watching though.

It wouldn't make the morning go any faster. John turned away from his own pictures and started going back through some files.

The inspirational pieces in the Grateful column kept catching his eye. He called them that for lack of a better term. They weren't religious, not preachy in the least, but they were uplifting. Somehow, they made him want to believe in God and trust Him in a way he never had before.

His instincts told him that they would have the same impact on other readers, and he wondered if the author would be interested in a regular column—if he could find out who it was.

That was something else he would talk to Grace about.

A few hours later, he had pulled together enough for another issue of the paper. His editorial page would be easy that week. He would simply introduce—or reintroduce—himself.

At twelve fifteen, John decided he couldn't wait any longer. If he called now, he might be able to catch Grace before she ate. He could even treat her to lunch. His lackluster sandwich could linger in the fridge for another day.

Renee answered the phone sounding reasonably professional, but as soon as she recognized John's voice, her tone changed to one of intimate curiosity. John could picture her leaning her elbows on the receptionist desk, getting ready for a good gossip session.

"I haven't seen you in here for a few days," she said. "Do you need another appointment or…?" She let the question hang.

"I wondered if I could speak with Grace Severight," John asked, willing patience into his voice. "If she's not busy with a client," he added hurriedly.

"I think she's free. Just one moment."

John breathed a sigh of relief that Renee wasn't going to persist with unwanted conversation. He supposed she was a nice enough young woman, just not his style.

Not like Grace…

No, he really had to get a grip on himself. He wasn't looking for anyone to be his style.

"John?" Grace's voice came on the phone. Unless he was reading too much into things, she sounded glad that it was him.

"I was going to call you," she rushed on. "I have some good news."

"Did you hear from the daycare?" he asked.

He could visualize the light in her eyes and the warmth of her pleased smile as he listened intently to her share the details of Toby's acceptance into the daycare.

"That's fantastic," he said. "I'm so happy it worked out."

"Thank you," Grace said. "There will be some adjustments, but it will be worth it."

"Definitely."

There was a beat of silence, and John wondered if he was the first person she'd shared the news with. He couldn't help hoping that he was.

"I have news too," he said, "but I was wondering if you had plans for lunch?"

"Well, now that you've got me curious," Grace teased in a way that made his skin tingle, "I'm going to have to say that I don't have any plans for lunch."

"Do you want to meet at Murphy's?" he suggested.

"You're starting to sound like you've always lived here," Grace said. "You're getting to be a regular there."

"We can go somewhere else if you'd prefer," John said. He stopped himself from adding that he just wanted to be with her.

"To be honest," Grace said, "I'd planned on taking a short lunch and then leaving early to go to Adventures in Learning to sign some papers."

John tried not to notice his heart sinking like a boulder, weighted with disappointment.

"I actually packed my lunch, and I was going to just drive to the park or something. Why don't I pick you up?"

"That would be great," John said. "I'm at *The Chronicle*. I'll bring the sandwich I made."

A short time later, they were having a mini picnic on a bench in Caledon Park.

"Do you remember this park?" Grace asked, taking a banana out of her lunch bag and inspecting it for bruises. "I mean, from when you lived here before?"

"Yes," John said, not adding anything else. There were some people he wanted to discourage conversation with, but never with Grace. Still, he wasn't keen on taking a rocky trip down memory lane.

She stirred and frowned a little, and he was afraid that he had ruined this brief interlude in her busy day.

"It can't have been easy to come back after you've been away for a while. My friend Jenny Powell—well, now it's Hart—went through an adjustment when she moved back to care for her grandmother."

"I met Jenny," John said, his muscles relaxing. "I went into the grocery store to buy some fruit for my lunch. That's one of the things I wanted to tell you."

He held the apple up like an offering.

"She's a good friend of mine," Grace said. "We should get together with her and her husband. David is a great guy. I think you'd like him." She went suddenly quiet and appeared intently interested in her bagel. Her hair was pulled back, and he could see that the tips of her ears were flushed.

"I'm sure I would," John said quietly.

"Sorry," Grace mumbled.

"What for?"

"I shouldn't try to plan things like we're…" *Dating? A couple?*

"I wouldn't mind meeting your friends," John said, even as he warned himself that she was right to put the brakes on whatever it was before either of them had false expectations.

Grace chewed and swallowed the last of her bagel, cleaned her hands on a wet wipe and checked the time.

"You said you had a couple of things to tell me?" She offered John a wet wipe as he finished his own sandwich. The apple and the banana remained untouched.

"Yes," he said, "I've decided that I would like to teach photography for those sessions you were telling me about. If you still want me," he added. He was a little hesitant after seeing how troubled her face had looked after she mentioned them hanging out with Jenny and David.

"Of course I do," she said, standing up and clapping her hands together. "I'll have to fill you in on some things, and we'll make some decisions, like whether you'll be teaching different age groups and how that'll work."

She took her garbage to a nearby receptacle, and John followed. She continued chatting as they walked to her car.

"There are actually some adult and children art classes on tonight. One of Michelle's friends is an artist, and she helped me make arrangements to bring him in. You should come. It would give you a chance to see the setup and meet some people."

"Doesn't this all get expensive?" John asked. "Bringing people in, I mean? I wouldn't feel right about charging you."

The last thing he was doing this for was the money.

"We'll work that out," Grace said hurriedly. "We take donations, and most of the people we get in to lead sessions are happy to have a chance to publicize what they do. So, will you come tonight?" she asked again as they got to her car.

There were many things to consider before answering. John didn't want to get too attached to this town he'd left—or have anyone get too attached to him. Despite helping the newspaper get back on its feet again, he wasn't going to let his roots grow too deep. He didn't want to set up false hopes in Toby or in anyone else.

He wasn't going to be a regular participant in town events. Looming like a persistent darkness in the background was also the thought that there was a fairly significant chance he could run into his father.

But looking down into Grace's hope-filled face, there was only one answer he could give.

"I'll be there."

Chapter Ten

Grace and Toby were running a bit late to the art class. They had narrowly avoided a meltdown when they couldn't find his camera, which he now insisted on taking everywhere with him. They'd retrieved it from where it had somehow been jostled off his dresser and become lodged between that and the bed, and she was now urging him into the car.

She didn't want John to arrive at the center and her not be there to greet him, especially since she was the one who had talked him into coming.

She had realized after their brief lunch date—*No, not date*, she corrected herself—after their lunch together, that she hadn't told him about the call from Blanche Collins, the social worker. She wondered if that had been an unconscious but somehow deliberate choice.

She just knew, with an aching certainty, that

talking about the possibility that it could happen wasn't going to make her feel any better.

She had been like that her whole life. While it seemed that others couldn't wait to confide in their friends, telling each and every detail of the ups and downs of their lives, Grace often found the input of others confusing and contradictory rather than helpful. She had always preferred to mediate and muddle through things on her own—with the Lord's help, of course.

Even when she was drinking, it hadn't made her become sloppy and embarrassingly open. Instead, she had felt more gathered into herself, not only to keep the secret, but because it was her problem to work through. Once she'd realized it was a problem, of course.

Even in her support group, for which she had much gratitude, she wasn't inclined to share much. She certainly didn't think that she was better than anyone else; it just wasn't her style.

So why did she want to share so much with John and care about what he thought?

Blanche had made it sound like Toby's eventual return to his mother was inevitable. Grace knew how wrong it would be to pray that somehow Tiffany would slip up again... Well, she wouldn't think about it. For now, she would focus on the present and enjoy every moment she had with Toby.

Who knew how quickly it would come about anyway? Blanche would be exceedingly careful and wouldn't rush into any decisions. Grace felt slightly better, even knowing how strong an advocate the social worker was for children being with their natural parents.

The bottom line was that they were all striving toward the common goal of Toby being safe and happy.

The foyer behind the double doors was alive with energy and chatter. As always, when she stepped into a crowd, Grace took time for a deep breath and a prayer. She was grateful for the seed of an idea that had been planted in her mind, but she was infinitely more grateful for God's spirit and for the talents and efforts of everyone who kept the programs growing and thriving.

Her eyes sought out John in the people milling around, and she saw him chatting with Jenny and David Hart.

He looked slightly too big and rugged for his surroundings, and he wore a shy expression that belied his ruggedness and caused a pitter-patter in Grace's heart. His hair had a slicked-down look, and he had shaved again. She tried to decide if she liked him this way best or when he was a bit wild and unkempt...

Her cheeks flamed, and she cleared her throat and turned her attention to Toby.

"Look, there's…" she started to say, but Toby was way ahead of her and raced toward John.

"Toby, be careful," she called, following after him. "Watch that you don't bump into anyone."

"You made it," John said. The spark in his eyes when he looked at her made Grace glad she had taken the time to put on a touch of makeup and was wearing a burnt-orange sweater that flattered her coloring.

"Sorry I'm a bit late," she said, "but I see you're doing okay." She greeted Jenny and David.

"Great to see you," David said and smiled while Jenny greeted her with a hug.

"Are you doing the art session? Are the girls here?" Grace asked.

"We sure are," Jenny said. She pointed to her twin stepdaughters, Rowe and Reba, now nine years old and chatting with a group of their friends.

"Carson is with David's parents," Jenny added, referring to their beautiful little boy and newest member of their family. "They love a chance to spoil him."

"The twins are getting so grown-up," Jenny commented.

It was especially noticeable in Reba, who

thankfully was in remission from cancer. She was taller and had put a healthy amount of weight back on, and her light brown hair was thick and shiny.

"You must be so thankful," Grace said and was caught off guard by the wistfulness in her own voice.

"I am," Jenny said. "Are you and John…?"

Grace shook her head rapidly, sending a hurried glance in John's direction, but he appeared to be deep in conversation with David.

David Hart, a family counselor and all-around nice guy, was always easy to talk to, and Grace was glad he was here.

"John was one of my patients. Now he's… Well, he's been helping Toby learn how to take pictures, and he's… He might teach photography for a session. He's really very good." She heard a note of insistence come into her voice as she grappled to define who or what John was to her.

Jenny lightly stroked her arm and smiled. "I know who John Bishop is, Grace. I do some part-time writing for the paper, remember? There's practically a shrine to his photographs there. And even if there wasn't, his work has been in quite a few magazines and other places. I wasn't trying to hit a sensitive spot, so I'm sorry if I came across as nosy." She wrinkled her nose. "Even though the truth is that I *am* nosy."

They chuckled together. "That's okay," Grace said. "I guess you could say that John is someone I'm getting to know."

The awkward moment passed, and she was glad when they were ushered into the classroom where the art teacher waited. They sat near the Harts, but Grace counted on them all getting absorbed in the project, which was to paint a bird in a vivid color while it sat on a stark black branch against a white background.

"Your eyes should be drawn to the bird," the instructor said. "It's a symbol of the beauty of creation."

While painstakingly following instructions, Grace struggled not to become too absorbed in thoughts about John. He smelled fresh and woodsy, and she noticed that despite having large hands, he had fingers that were tapered, almost elegant-looking. A little while into the class, it became clear that his creative talents easily followed him from the camera to the canvas.

She almost wished that Toby was sitting between them, instead of on her other side. Almost...but not quite.

As for her own work, she wouldn't bet that anyone would be able to separate it from five-year-old Toby's in a lineup.

John leaned closer to her, and she resisted the urge to put her hands up to cover her work. But he didn't have anything to say about it.

Instead, he said in a lowered tone that caused every nerve in her to light up with alertness, "I like your friends."

It was the kind of thing she could imagine people who had started to date saying to each other. But that probably wasn't how he meant it.

What was wrong with her tonight? Her thoughts were running all over the place.

"Look at my painting, John." Toby leaned across her to put his artwork in front of John.

"This is great, bud," John said. "I really like how you used color on the bird."

"I like yours too," Toby said graciously.

John used the opportunity to start explaining the way a person could find and use contrasting colors when setting up a photograph, and Grace listened intently, glad to have something to focus on other than her futile crush—which she was willing to admit she had—and also because listening to someone talk about what they loved was sheer pleasure.

In the latter part of the class, the instructor walked around to look at their work and make suggestions. Grace mustered her self-control and did not make an excuse to bolt from the room.

She knew she needed to take more risks, even

though *not* taking risks and having a productive, orderly life was how she managed to get by. It was how she went moment by moment, not only to avoid falling prey to alcohol again, but to avoid allowing herself to think that there was something—or someone—missing in her life.

She was afraid that if she went down the path of self-pity, she might never find her way back.

The instructor picked up her work and studied it. Grace consciously tried not to hold her breath and refrained from making excuses for her work.

She tried to tell herself this was supposed to be fun. That's what she would tell anyone else. She sensed John also waiting to hear what would be said about her work, and while she appreciated his interest, part of her wished that he would just go away.

The instructor's black hair fell to his shoulders, and his eyes gave Grace the sensation that he had experienced a lot. Maybe art had helped him to deal with at least some of it.

Like John and Toby.

"I like what you've done here," he said, his voice soothing and genuine. "But there's a sense of holding back. Don't hold back. There's no reason to. People are always going to judge us for one reason or another, so we should always be true to ourselves and go for it."

Why did it suddenly feel like he was talking about more than her painting?

Grace felt like she'd just gotten off a rapidly spinning ride at the town fair and was staggering to regain her footing. This evening had her off-kilter.

"Interesting evening," John said as they tidied up their supplies. "I'm glad I came."

"Me too," Grace said. His words calmed her and reminded her why she had invited him in the first place.

"I'll show you around if you have time," she said. "There's a lot more to see. This was the main activity going on tonight, but there are always other regular sessions."

"I'd like that," John said.

The Hart family came over then. The twins made a fuss over Toby, who looked torn between basking in it and bolting.

"Would you all like to come for supper at our place this Friday night?" Jenny said.

Grace tugged at her ear, hoping that John didn't think she had asked her friends to invite them like they were some kind of couple. She knew Jenny always meant well, but she hoped she wasn't getting any ideas about matchmaking. That seemed to be a side effect of anyone who found themselves in a blissfully happy marriage or relationship.

Grace wanted to say yes. She'd been meaning to socialize more. Life couldn't be all about work, after all. But she didn't want to say yes like she was agreeing for both of them.

"I mean, that sounds good to me…" she waffled and looked at John.

The stony expression on his face seemed to indicate that he thought it was a bad idea—a very bad idea.

Grace's throat thickened, and her face grew warm.

"Hi there, George," David said, and Grace realized that John probably wasn't even thinking about the invitation that Jenny had extended.

No, he was watching his father's approach the way he might watch a poisonous snake slithering in a slow but determined way toward him.

John had known it was possible they'd see his father here. Knowing that something was possible and mentally preparing for it was entirely different than being faced with the actual fact. It was like being awoken by a fire alarm in the middle of the night. Having knowledge that buildings did catch fire in no way took away the fear and shock when it happened.

Watching his father walk toward their group, John's mouth went dry, and he felt a slight tremor in his hands. He clenched them into fists.

George did look good, he reluctantly admitted to himself. It was easier—more distancing—to think of him as George.

He was clean-shaven, his posture was good and his hair combed neatly. He wore a brown suit. His eyes, though holding an anxious expression, were clear, and they met John's directly, with no shiftiness.

A memory drifted into John's mind of someone—maybe someone from church? He couldn't remember—who had said that John had his father's eyes.

What? Bloodshot and can barely keep them open?

For the first time, he could see the likeness.

Jenny and David were talking to George like they knew him and actually liked him. One of the twins, the one with brown eyes like her father, was teaching Toby a hand-clapping game. No one was aware that he was a spool of black thread about to unravel at the slightest pull.

But then he felt warm fingers gently squeezing his arm, and he turned to see Grace. She had a look in her eyes that was both cautious and encouraging.

Encouraging what?

He didn't know what she expected of him, but he was already quite sure he wouldn't be able to deliver.

"Hello...son." George's greeting was soft, tentative. "It's good to see you here."

John nodded tersely. A flurry of angry words chilled at the edge of his tongue. The urge to spew them out second only to the urge to turn and walk away. But both of those urges were overcome by the awareness that there were other people, including children, present.

And he didn't want to do anything that would upset Grace.

He rooted around for something noncommittal to say, something that would sound okay to the people around them, while letting his father know that there was no way they were doing the not-so-happy reunion thing here.

"I enjoyed the art class," he said, thinking that even that felt too revealing.

"It was really interesting," Grace chimed in. John could hear the relief in her voice. "The instructor was great, very patient and encouraging. I learned a lot, though I can't say that I'll be giving up my day job to become an artist."

"I won't either," Jenny said, and John realized that their supper invitation was hanging in the air unanswered. He felt bad about that, but there was no way he was going to respond to it with his father standing right here. Besides, he wished he had a better read on how Grace felt about them going for supper together.

"Invitation is still open," David said as he waved Rowe and Reba over. "Talk it over with Grace and get back to us."

John noted that he had kept his voice low, as if he sensed that John wouldn't appreciate being put on the spot. David Hart was a good guy, and John looked forward to getting to know him better.

If his father didn't live here, he could see himself putting down roots and not thinking about when and where his next move was going to be.

Through the roaring rush that was the present state of his churning thoughts, he was aware of Grace saying goodbye to the Harts and saying they would for sure finalize supper plans.

Did that mean she was willing to go? Did she consider it a date? How would he feel about it if she did?

"John's picture was fantastic," she said to George. "You would have thought he'd been painting his whole life."

"John has always had a gift."

Hearing his father make such a calm and confident declaration was enough to bring John back to the reality of how desperately he wanted to get away from him.

But at the same time, he was trying to remember if he'd ever heard his father give him a compliment—a real compliment, not the flattery-laden wheedling he did when he needed something that usually had to do with him feeding his addiction.

John didn't want to need those words, but there was no denying that the small boy inside of him still did. How different things might have been—how differently he might feel toward his father—if George had only taken the time to let his family know that he loved and treasured them.

"He is extremely talented," Grace agreed. "And he's generous with his talent too. He's been teaching Toby how to take pictures."

Toby had returned to her side, and Grace lightly touched his shoulder for a moment. Toby tilted his head and again looked astonishingly like Simon.

Can he see it too?

That snapped John out of wistfully rewriting the past. He wasn't going to stand here while his estranged father and his—whatever Grace was to him—discussed his merits.

But he wouldn't walk away without acknowledging Toby. He couldn't do that.

He leaned down to the little boy. "You did a great job today, bud. I'm looking forward to taking more pictures with you, because we both learned so much today, didn't we?"

Toby nodded happily.

"John," George said, "before you go, I'd love it if we…"

But with or without Toby and Grace here, John was at his breaking point.

"I have to go," he said. He stopped himself from adding that he was sorry.

He was sure he could feel Grace's gaze, along with his father's, on him as he walked away.

The next evening, as he ate some leftover pasta at the Russells' kitchen table, he wondered if or how he could have handled the situation differently.

He'd gotten into the habit of reading the Bible while staying at the motel and was starting to give serious consideration to buying one. In the meantime, he was surprisingly happy to find that the Russells had left one out for easy access. He assumed it was just their habit, because they had no reason to have done so for his benefit. But he chose to think that it was a sign for him to continue exploring.

Even with his limited exposure, what he had quickly discovered was that love and forgiveness were key messages in the Bible. That fact was pretty much impossible to ignore.

The question was, what was he willing and able to do with that knowledge? Every time he tried to think about forgiving his parents, memories of neglect and abuse came rushing in, suffocating any light that was trying to break through.

He raked his fingernails along the side of his face. Maybe he shouldn't have said yes to staying, even for a short time.

But he had made commitments to *The Chronicle* and to Grace, and he had made a promise to himself to protect Grace and Toby from his father. He *had* to make Grace understand that the man was not to be trusted. As tempting as it was, he couldn't leave.

His phone rang, and he could see that it was Grace. For a split second, he considered not answering. He had no desire to discuss the brief meeting with his father, and he didn't care to hear what she thought about him walking out.

But it might be about Toby, or…or it might be that he always wanted to talk to her for whatever reason.

"Hi, Grace."

"Hi, I'm sorry to bother you."

"You're not bothering me." *You could never bother me.* She didn't sound like she wanted to lecture him. She sounded…nervous?

"How are things with you?" John asked when a pause lingered. "Everything okay with Toby?"

"Yes, we're both good. I'm calling because— well, I think it's only polite that we get an answer to Jenny and David. Are you interested in going for supper?"

He was suddenly giddy with relief. "I would love to go for supper."

"Okay, that's great," she said. "I mean, it's good. They'll be pleased."

"Yeah, it should be a good time."

"I'm going to suggest six thirty," Grace said. "Is that okay for you?"

"That's great with me, but isn't that a little late for Toby's supper? Not that I'm questioning your parenting skills," he quickly added.

"No, I don't mind you asking," Grace said, her voice softening. "It's nice of you to think of Toby. But I'm going to give him an early supper, and then he'll watch a movie with the girls in a different room. It will just be us grown-ups, at least for a good part of the evening."

John sensed that she was checking to make sure that was okay with him without making too big a deal out of it.

"Okay. Sounds good," he repeated.

"Do you want me to pick you up?" Grace offered.

She always had such an independent spirit, John mused, smiling to himself. But there was one thing he was sure of in the midst of all the confusion about his father, the decisions he had made, and even about Grace herself. He didn't want her to ever feel like he wasn't willing to make an effort for her.

"No," he said. "I'll pick you up."

Chapter Eleven

It was ridiculous to be so keyed up over dinner with friends.

She didn't have a large number of friends, but she trusted that the ones she had were loyal, and she showed them the same loyalty. She had a profession that she was passionate about. She thanked God every day for the chance to do something she loved to do and that truly helped others.

And she had Toby. That thought caused an acute ache. After Blanche Collins's phone call, she had no idea how much longer she would have him. She told herself several times a day that all she could do was continue to love him as well as she could.

She squared her shoulders and gave her reflection one last inspection. She thought she looked okay. Her blouse blended the colors of a setting sun, and her black jeans were freshly pressed. She thought she perhaps looked a bit softer and more anxious than usual.

Grace spun away from the mirror as the fluttering in her stomach renewed in double time.

She had never been the type to base her life and her decisions around what others might think, so why did she so badly want John to think she looked pretty tonight?

When she was interviewed to be Toby's foster mother—and researched what it might take for her to permanently adopt him—she had wanted them to know what they were getting. She'd been open and honest about being single and how she didn't anticipate that changing.

She'd set out to prove that she could and would be everything needed to give Toby the best possible chance at a good life.

When she tried to imagine their future together now, she couldn't visualize it without John there too, teaching him and helping him along.

"Toby." She went to his room. He tugged down the sweater she'd asked him to put on and added his constant companion, his camera, around his neck.

Grace knew that once he started at the new daycare, he wouldn't be able to take the camera with him every day. The staff would justifiably be concerned about something happening to it. But she still didn't have the heart to ask him to leave it behind. She hoped that soon it would be his decision to leave it behind at times.

"Are you almost ready?" she asked him. "John will be here soon."

She approached him and smoothed down a cowlick. He squirmed but didn't back away as he used to.

"I'm itchy," he complained. "This sweater itches."

"Did you put on an undershirt like I told you?"

Toby shook his head.

"Do it quick, then. I'll help you."

John was punctual and rang the doorbell just as Grace finished tying Toby's shoes. She hurriedly slid her feet into her own shoes.

When Grace opened the door to greet John, a blast of cool autumn air reminded her that they were now in September, and she could no longer pretend that summer lingered. Before she knew it, she would be digging out her winter boots. The way Toby was growing, he would soon need new boots.

But it might not be me buying them.

She never cried in public—she rarely even cried in private—but she felt a dangerous stinging behind her eyes, which she rapidly blinked away.

All she would think about tonight was enjoying dinner with friends—old and new.

John had clearly taken time with his own appearance. He was freshly shaven again, and he wore a button-down shirt with a collar. Something about its starched look made Grace wonder if he'd bought it especially for the occasion. The thought made her slightly giddy.

"You look very nice," he said quietly, the appreciation in his eyes backing up the compliment.

"So do you."

Toby hoisted his camera and took a picture of them.

Grace wanted to see that picture, to see her and John captured in a moment.

But that was silly.

"Shall we go?"

John offered his hand to help her down the steps, just like a proper date. Toby clung to her other hand.

She suddenly ached for family and permanence in a way she had never experienced before. It was probably just the thought of having to surrender Toby back to his mother.

As John reached the bottom of the steps first, she caught his gaze and had the strangest sensation that he was aching for the same thing.

Even in autumn, it was hard not to think of the home where Jenny and David lived as Christmas House. It had a well-deserved reputation for holiday cheer during the Christmas season.

It had been owned for years by Jenny's grandparents. Her grandfather had been deceased for years, and now that her grandmother was settled in a senior-care home, Jenny and David carried on the tradition of opening up the house to friends and family for the holiday season.

She wondered how much Toby would remember about it from last year and was already excited at the prospect of sharing it with him again.

Every time she thought about Toby, she also thought about losing him. Once again, Grace reminded herself to focus on the evening ahead.

"I remember this house," John said as they got out of the car.

"Did you visit it often?" Grace asked.

An expression crossed his face that suggested there could be a great deal to say about that.

"Not too often" was all he said.

One day, maybe she would hear all about John's years growing up. Maybe she could try to understand his animosity toward his father. Then again, maybe some things couldn't be explained to others.

That was another reason she didn't like to talk about her drinking and didn't even like to share in group all that much. Even after considerable introspection, she couldn't come up with the reason why she'd been driven to drink the way she had. She just was.

"Come on in!" Jenny threw open the door, and the scent of a savory dish wafted out to entice their noses.

"Something smells delicious," John said.

"It's Gran's tried-and-true Crock-Pot chili recipe," Jenny said. "I thought it was the perfect night for it. It's really starting to feel like fall out there, isn't it?"

Everyone expressed agreement, and David stepped forward to take their coats and usher them in.

"Besides," Jenny added breezily, "it's a no-muss, no-fuss kind of recipe, and I'd rather spend time with our guests than be too preoccupied in the kitchen. Carson went to bed without a fuss too."

"Aww, I'll have to give him snuggles next time," Grace said.

Jenny Hart was one of the few classmates who knew that Grace had sought help to stop drinking. They had talked after a Christmas Eve service one night before Jenny and David were married. They had used the time to confess some of their fears and secrets. She'd put her trust in Jenny and had never regretted it.

Grace knew what most people might think when they were told someone was an alcoholic—

stumbling around, slurring their words, perhaps drinking until they were sick—and because they had never seen Grace do any of those things, they would never have put that label on her.

No, she was always the responsible one, cleaning up in the kitchen at parties—and sneaking drinks while she did it.

She glanced John's way. He and David were laughing about something like a couple of guys who'd been buddies for a long time.

She wondered if he would have been able to see through her facade.

Could he now?

No, he had made his hatred for alcohol abusers clear. The fact that he couldn't find forgiveness in his heart toward his father was something for him and God to work out. She cared for John and was grateful for what he was doing for Toby, but she would certainly never give him the opportunity to judge her.

Rowena and Reba came out of their bedrooms to greet Toby.

"Ready for a movie?" Rowe, the more outgoing of the twins, asked.

"We have two we think you might like," kind and quiet Reba added. "You can pick."

Toby put a finger in his mouth and rolled his eyes toward Grace.

"You know these girls," Grace said. "You

don't have to be shy. He was excited at home," she told the others.

"Getting twin-teamed can be a little intimidating for anyone," David said drolly. "Whatever Toby is comfortable with, we're good with. He can stay with us while we eat, and maybe he'll want to join the girls later."

"No, I want to see the movie…please," Toby spoke up clearly, and Grace exhaled a proud-parent breath.

The twins each took him by one hand and escorted him down the hall and downstairs into a newly renovated rumpus room.

Grace was happy that Toby had pushed past his social awkwardness to speak up for himself and hadn't let fear stop him from doing something fun that he probably would have regretted missing.

That was something she definitely needed to keep in mind.

Soon the four adults were settled around the kitchen table. Grace sat beside John, and that intangible but warm and soothing something emanated from her.

John wanted to reach beneath the table and squeeze her hand. Instead, he took in his surroundings with a practiced but appreciative eye.

A house this size could easily seem too vast

and formal, more like a place you would visit rather than live in. But Jenny's love for the home and comfortable attachment to it showed in the kitchen table made of wood and scuffed with use, and in the warm, vibrant colors she had chosen for the decor.

"I love your kitchen," Grace said, and John again felt that spark of kinship between them.

"It's so inviting," they said at the same time, and all four of them laughed.

"Just how much time *have* you been spending together?" David teased.

John waited for Grace to protest that they were just friends, but she smiled like whatever they were didn't need an explanation, so he stilled his habitual instinct to protest any mention of a relationship.

"But seriously," Jenny said, "I'm glad you like the kitchen. I know the dining room is nicer for guests but…"

"But we're not guests," Grace finished for her. "We're friends."

We're friends.

John hadn't wanted to get too sentimental when Grace asked him if he remembered this house, but to him, it had always carried the bittersweet tang of something he wanted and something he knew he would never have: home, safety, companionship.

Except now he was inside the home, with a woman who intrigued and challenged him even though he couldn't say exactly what they were to each other. The term *friend* seemed both too presumptuous for the short time they had been acquainted yet also too plain for the unexpected and undeniable sparks that flared up between them.

They were with people who'd welcomed John into this home like it was the most natural thing in the world to do. Downstairs, there was a little boy who tugged at his heartstrings. At first it had been because he reminded him of Simon, but more and more, it was because he reminded John of his younger self.

He was profoundly glad that because of someone like Grace, Toby would get a much better start than he'd had.

"Who's hungry for chili?" Jenny asked, bringing the Crock-Pot right over to the table and carefully setting it down on a place mat in the middle of it. "David, would you say the blessing, please?"

It felt like the most natural thing in the world to sit beside Grace as David prayed over their food. Years ago, when he had gone to church, he could remember seeing couples or families holding hands as they prayed. He had longed for that kind of intimacy, until he'd learned to slam the door on those kinds of yearnings.

Until now.

Now he imagined what it would be like to be able to hold Grace's hand as they prayed together.

"Amen," David said.

"Amen," John echoed faintly, embarrassed that he had let his thoughts wander.

"Dig in," Jenny said. "We're not much on formalities here."

Soon they were all spooning up chili and exclaiming over its delicious flavors.

"Is that brown sugar I taste?" John asked.

"Just a smidge," Jenny said. "Wow, I'm impressed."

"Me too." Grace half turned in her chair and gave him a slow, studying smile that warmed his stomach and worked up to flush his cheeks.

"So, you cook?" she asked him.

"I get by," he said.

"Did your mom teach you?" Jenny asked.

"Or your dad?" David followed up.

"I basically taught myself," John said. He could hear an abruptness coming into his tone, and he saw tension tighten Grace's mouth. He wasn't going to ruin their evening, but the questions were leading in a direction he did not want to go.

"George did bring a pretty mean chili to a church potluck a couple of weeks ago," David said.

John forced a smile. "I'm sure he did. So, changing the subject, what movie are the kids watching?"

They began to chat about movie choices and how difficult it could be these days to find something that the whole family could watch.

As if he had ever had movie time with his family...

But at least they weren't talking about his parents anymore.

Throughout the rest of the meal, he could sense a slight anxiety radiating from Grace, although she did keep up her end of the conversation.

Many years ago, John made himself a promise that he wasn't going to let his father ruin any more of his life. Now George wasn't even here, but somehow, his presence lingered. John needed to get him out of his head if he was going to enjoy the rest of the evening.

"Who would like to take dessert downstairs?" Jenny offered. "We can see how the kids are getting along."

"That sounds great," Grace said. "Let me help you clean up the supper dishes."

"I wouldn't think of it. David will help me

later. Dessert is apple pie, but confession time, I didn't make it. It is from Graham's, though, so I can vouch for its deliciousness. Who wants ice cream?"

She called the offer of dessert downstairs to where the twins and Toby were watching the movie, and enthusiastic acceptance was shouted back up the stairs.

"I *will* help you serve those," Grace insisted, "and carry them downstairs."

It was in Grace's nature to help, John noted. It was a great gift, and it filled his heart with gratitude. But it also frightened him a little. He did not want to start counting on her or on anyone. The mere mention of his father's name was enough to remind him that it was better if he stayed on the move as much as he could, not putting down roots and not having people count on him any more than he wanted to count on them.

"Do you want to talk more about your parents sometime?" Grace asked quietly as he stood beside her at the counter dishing out ice cream.

He smiled a thank-you for the offer but shook his head. They carried the desserts downstairs and saw that Toby was sandwiched between Rowe and Reba.

He raised his little face like John was the one person he'd been waiting for and asked, "How come the picture is all blurry like that?"

"It's because it shows that she's remembering something that happened a long time ago," Reba explained, trying to be helpful.

But John knew what the question was really about. He too had wanted to know everything a camera could do.

"The picture is what we call out of focus, Toby. And like Reba said, they're using that technique to show you that what's happening is different from the rest of the story. Next time we take pictures together, I'll show you."

Next time.

Toby nodded with relief.

But nothing had to be permanent, John reminded himself. Even when his traitorous heart was telling him he might want it to be.

Near the close of the evening, the four adults were back upstairs chatting compatibly about a variety of light topics. When Jenny mentioned that she occasionally wrote articles for *The Chronicle* and also wrote devotions for some church publications, John perked up.

"I don't know if you'll tell me this," he said, "but are you by chance the person who writes Grateful?"

Jenny sighed. "I wish," she said. "No, I don't know who it is, but as acting editor, you should have access to the contact information of anyone who contributes to the paper."

"Vivian did give me a list," John mused.

Grace checked the time. "This has been so fun," she said. "But I think I'd better get Toby home to bed."

At the door, they exchanged goodbyes and promises to do it again soon.

"Let me cook next time," Grace said.

John was glad that Toby's bedtime prevented Grace from trying to question him further on how easily a pleasant evening could have edged into a near disaster because of mention of his father.

Yet, as he drove home, he thought how easy it would be to get caught up in life here. In Grace's and Toby's lives. In the lives of their friends who were readily including him in their future plans.

Sudden and profound confusion washed over him, causing an ache and a helplessness that even his injured ankle hadn't.

John let himself into the Russells' house and took some deep breaths. He knew he had better find something else to focus on.

After pouring a glass of milk, he sat at the kitchen table, opened his laptop and pulled up the list of contacts Vivian had emailed him.

The last phone number and email on the list caused his swallow of milk to lodge and thicken in his throat.

They belonged to his father.

Chapter Twelve

All the paperwork was filled out and signed, and on the third Monday in September, Grace dropped Toby off at Adventures in Learning.

She helped Toby unbuckle his seat belt, her own fingers clumsy with anxiety. No matter how much she had tried to pray and prepare, no matter her trust in Ruby Kaiswatum's and her staff's kindness and expertise, scars of the previous daycare's inability to embrace and accept Toby still remained.

But she wouldn't—not for anything in the world—let Toby see her concern. She told herself what she often told her patients. *Everything is going to be okay. It might not be what you expect, but it will be okay.*

These weren't just flippant words to her. They were something she had learned through painful trials and long nights of prayer.

"Ready, bud?"

Toby's hair was slicked down. He wore a navy

blue pullover with long sleeves, as the weather warranted, and a freshly pressed pair of jeans.

He looked great, but the anxiety in his eyes mirrored hers, and Grace opened her arms, not touching him but letting him decide whether or not to accept the embrace. He collapsed into her, and her arms went around him. She breathed in the scent of the baby shampoo she had used on his fine hair the night before.

"You're going to do just great," she murmured into his ear. "Everyone here is going to love you."

He pulled back and peered into her face. "As much as you and John do?"

Her heart fractured, and each splinter had a different lament. Toby now understood that she loved him. Would he still understand that if and when he went back to his mother? He knew that John also loved him—Grace believed that too—but did that mean he thought of them as a pair? Did he assume they would always be together in his life?

"Welcome, Toby!" The warm voice of Ruby Kaiswatum floated out to them. It had a calming effect on Grace, and she prayed the same for Toby.

"We are so happy you are here." The woman offered Toby her hand.

He hesitated and looked back at Grace, who nodded encouragement.

"You're coming too, right?" he asked.

"Yes, but just for a little while," Grace said. She repeated what she had told him last night. "I will come in, and Ms. Kaiswatum and her helpers will get you settled. When you're feeling comfortable, I'll leave and go to work. But I'm going to leave work early today and for the rest of this week, so you'll see me at four o'clock. Do you remember what that looks like on the clock?"

Toby nodded, but his fingernails went into his mouth for a good gnawing session, and he still hadn't taken Ms. Kaiswatum's hand.

Grace noticed that the other woman did not appear surprised or concerned about this. Instead, she asked, "Toby, do you remember the names of the hamsters you met the first time you came here?"

A small spark of interest began to replace the concern in Toby's eyes.

"Romeo and Juliet?" he said.

"That's exactly right," Ms. Kaiswatum said, praising him. "You have a great memory. Would you like to see them again?"

He looked back at Grace. He didn't take Ms. Kaiswatum's hand, but he did begin to follow her into the school.

"If I had my camera," he said to Grace, "I could take pictures of Romeo and Juliet and show John."

Grace tensed slightly. It had taken some negotiating to get him to agree to leave the camera at home. She had been determined that he understand the risks of something happening to it but didn't want to worry him so much that he never wanted to take it out or use it. As always, she hoped what she had done and said was right.

But it seemed that his remark was just that, a remark, and they continued to follow the daycare director into the facility.

It was clear to Grace after just a few minutes that the staff there knew exactly what they were doing. Soon Toby was engrossed in feeding the hamsters and getting praised for his efforts. She was filled with gratitude, but her contradictory feelings also stabbed a little hurt over Toby not seeming to mind when she had to leave. She mentally shook her head as she walked to her car and chuckled ruefully.

That had gone as well as, or better than, she ever could have anticipated, and she thanked God for that. But as she settled back into her car and let the deep quiet that followed a potentially difficult task descend over her, she realized that something else was now bubbling to the surface again.

She cared about John—more than she wanted
to—and she wanted to help him find a way to
forgive his father. All in all, they'd had a fun
time visiting with Jenny and David, and Toby
had reported that he thought the twins were really nice. But she couldn't shake the look on his
face when John's parents were mentioned. It had
been the face of a man who was holding burdens
of bitterness so tightly and for so long that they
might soon etch themselves into his heart, and
there would be no going back.

Grace had never blamed any hurt or drama
in her life for her drinking. She understood that
she was somehow genetically predisposed to it,
although neither of her parents were drinkers.
Like any other disease—because that's what it
was—it did not play favorites.

Understanding this certainly did not make not
drinking any easier. She knew that it was only
by throwing her burden on God daily, hourly,
that she refrained.

She also wondered, however, if she was rare
in not blaming her family or circumstances in
her life for her drinking. She'd certainly heard
countless stories in support groups of families
ripped apart, and the kind of bitterness that John
was clearly struggling to keep at bay.

But she had also witnessed these same people

let go of the resentments they were clinging to and find a way to forgive.

She wanted that for John. Yes, she knew it wasn't up to her, she couldn't make it happen, but she wanted it.

She was thankful to have a full quota of patients to focus on until her early departure. Even so, she struggled with the temptation to phone the daycare to check in...and to phone John.

She knew she shouldn't worry about not having heard from him since their dinner at the Harts'. She imagined he was busy with the paper, and they still had plenty of time to talk about him teaching photography, as other sessions were already scheduled for the upcoming weeks. But knowing she shouldn't worry in her head was entirely different from knowing it in her heart.

At four o'clock, Grace consciously made herself breathe as she approached the daycare. If Toby didn't do well here, she didn't know what she was going to do.

No, she wasn't going to think that way. The staff was highly skilled, kind and patient.

But what if Toby's mother didn't understand how important it was that Toby had the right environment to thrive in?

Usually foster parents and birth parents had more contact, but Tiffany's sole focus needed to be on getting herself clean and healthy and seeking treatment for her depression.

Once again, Grace handed her troubled thoughts over to the Lord. She could hardly encourage John to let his burdens go if she wasn't able to do so herself.

"Grace!" Toby ran toward her. But he didn't run with the desperation of a child at the end of a bad day seeking the comfort of the familiar. No, as he ran, his face was lit up with anticipation for all the things he wanted to share with her about his day.

"I take it he had a good day?" Grace asked a staff member whose name tag read Maegan.

The young woman grinned from ear to ear. "He had a *great* day."

As they drove home, Grace resolved that the next time she talked to Blanche Collins, she was going to tactfully challenge her on whether it really would be in Toby's best interest to be returned to his mother now that he was making significant progress. Even though Blanche said that the ultimate goal was to return the child to their natural parent, wasn't it—or shouldn't it be—the ultimate goal to do what was best for the child?

Stories about his day poured out of Toby as he stirred milk and a pudding mix for their dessert while she assembled burgers.

"I'm in charge of Romeo and Juliet for the whole entire week," he said, squaring back his shoulders and puffing out his chest. "I clean their cage every day, and I ask other kids to help me feed them."

"And the other kids want to help?" Grace asked.

"Oh, sure," he said breezily. "Everyone wants to feed them. The teachers say I should actchally keep an eye on that too, because it's not good for them to get too stuffed."

"No, I don't imagine it is." Grace tucked in a smile at his authoritative tone.

"So the other kids are nice?" She chewed her lip a bit, anxiously waiting for his answer.

"Yeah, they're nice."

His tone was a bit noncommittal, but at least he had no complaints. Then he launched into a description of artwork and pictures that were displayed around the room.

"Me and John could take better pictures too," he said with confidence. "Hey." He stopped, looking surprised at himself. "I didn't get my camera yet."

Grace considered suggesting that he wait until after supper, since he'd managed well so far without it. But he'd had such a successful day, and she could hardly see shy, troubled Toby in this chatty youngster. So instead, she said, "You can get it now if you want."

He hurried to his room and got it. He brought it into the kitchen to snap Grace's eyes watering as she chopped onion.

"Let's make sure no one sees these ones," she suggested.

"Don't worry, I'll tell everybody you weren't crying."

But their comfortable conversation made Grace feel like she might just cry.

She had just assured herself that Toby was asleep and was about to settle in with a collection of short stories by one of her favorite authors—an indulgence she rarely had time for these days—when her phone rang.

She snatched it up hastily. Even though once Toby was asleep, there was rarely anything but his troubled dreams that woke him, she didn't want to take any chances.

"Grace," a familiar voice said. "It's John. I hope it's okay for me to call now."

"Yes, yes, of course. I've been…" Grace paused briefly and then refused to censor herself. "I've been thinking about you today. To tell you the truth, I've been thinking about you since we had dinner with Jenny and David."

"I guess… I guess I'm glad to hear that."

She couldn't help laughing, although she

knew he hadn't meant to be funny. "I'll try not to be too flattered," she quipped.

Instead of laughter, there was a tense silence on the other end of the phone.

"John, what's wrong?" she prompted, gripping the phone.

"I wouldn't say there's anything wrong exactly," John said slowly. "I'm just… Well, I've come across something that I absolutely wasn't expecting, and I'm not sure what to do with the information."

"Okay, John, you're really confusing me. How can I help?" Grace's stomach somersaulted.

"I think I just need to talk it through with someone."

"What is it?" Grace asked. "What did you find out?"

Her mind shuffled possibilities, but she couldn't come up with anything feasible.

"Okay, you know how Jenny and I were talking about those anonymous uplifting articles that run in *The Chronicle* every so often?"

"Yes."

"I think… I think my father is the one who's writing them."

"I'm not sur—" That time, Grace did stop herself from saying that she wasn't surprised. She could easily imagine the George Bishop she knew writing those articles. But it was clear that

John's experience with his father was something completely different.

She might not agree with his refusal to forgive whatever it was he had to forgive. But she didn't have to agree; she only had to try to be a friend.

So the words were out of her mouth almost before she had finished her prayer.

"Do you want to ask him about it? If you do, I'll go with you."

Did John want to ask his father about the column? Did he want to ask the man he had virtually nothing but bad memories of if he was responsible for writing something that lifted his spirits?

John could barely get his head around it, let alone imagine a conversation.

And yet…if his father really had written those articles, John couldn't help but want to know how a man could possibly change that much.

He would do it for research.

Because any other reason would be unbearable.

It could also be a chance to talk honestly with Grace about what his father had put him through. He had never done that with anyone before—never wanted to do it—but the urge to protect her and Toby had only increased the more he spent time with them. Maybe it was time she knew what he knew.

Only a whisper of breath told him that Grace was still waiting for his answer.

"I might do that," John said. "Thanks for offering to go with me." He paused. "Grace?"

"Yes?"

He could picture her holding her phone, her gaze focused as it always was when she was determined to get an answer about something.

"I think it's important that we chat about my…fath—" He tried to say "father," but the word caught in his throat like a burr. He cleared his throat. "You and I need to talk about George. When are you free?"

"I could clear some time tomorrow afternoon," she said. "I could bring sandwiches to *The Chronicle*. What time do you take lunch?"

"Whenever you do," John said. "That's one of the advantages of running the show."

"I'll go in early," Grace said, thinking out loud as she rearranged her schedule. "I should be able to take a bit of a longer lunch if it's needed."

"I hate to put you out," John said. "But I wouldn't ask if I didn't think it was important."

"I think it's important too," Grace agreed. "Because I don't think you really know the person that George is."

"He's my father." This time, John got the word

out. Then he added in a voice as thin and sharp as a pin, "And it's you who doesn't know the type of person he is."

He didn't sleep at all well that night.

First of all, he was worried that he had created a boundary between himself and Grace by his remark on the phone about Grace not knowing his father. While he still believed that to be true, he would never question Grace's good sense and would never want her to think that he would.

She hadn't seemed offended, maybe a bit distracted more than anything. He wasn't sure how he felt about that either.

Finally, at about five in the morning, he gave up on sleep. Bleary-eyed, he got himself out of bed, put on a pot of coffee and popped a couple of pieces of whole wheat bread into the toaster.

If it wasn't so important that Grace understood exactly how dangerous trusting his father too much could be, he might have been able to see a certain dark humor in the situation. Both he and Grace were so stubborn, and they were both determined to prove themselves right in this situation.

As he sipped coffee and took a thoughtful bite out of a piece of toast, there was one simple fact that remained: Grace *didn't* know his father. There was no way she could, not the way he did.

There was no telling what George Bishop

wanted to drain from this small, trusting community, but John was sure it was something.

The only thing that didn't mesh, that he couldn't quite get his thoughts around, was that people who had known George from *before* seemed as willing as Grace to embrace him, to accept his facade as a good citizen.

But they didn't grow up with him as a father.

Surely there had to be some exceptions to this forgiveness rule. John found himself arguing with God over it. He was still struggling to believe God listened.

Despite rising early, the morning went quickly, and before he knew it, Grace had arrived, bringing sandwiches as promised.

When she walked in swinging a lunch kit and smiling, with her dark blond hair tumbling around her shoulders, John's limbs went light, as if her very presence drained away any of the dark memories that wanted to press down on him.

It occurred to him that she must have taken her hair out of its habitual work ponytail for their lunch break, and his heart was like a helium balloon as he considered the possible significance of this.

He had a sudden thought that if he could take one more photograph in his lifetime, he would use it to capture the way Grace Severight turned her head and smiled at him. The way her eyes radiated light and comfort. But he couldn't let undeniable attraction to her distract him from the things he needed to talk about.

After they had finished their sandwiches—delicious Black Forest ham with mustard and Swiss cheese on rye bread—John carefully folded his napkin, took a sip of his coffee and decided to start the difficult conversation with a question.

"How well do you know my father?"

He could see Grace considering her answer, her chin tightening a bit, like she was already getting ready to defend herself, or George, from a challenge.

"I would say that we are friendly acquaintances," Grace answered. She folded her own napkin, then unfolded it and repeated the actions.

John stayed quiet, waiting for her to elaborate.

"We run into each other at a number of events around town, and we are involved in many of the same activities," Grace said.

"What kind of activities?" John asked. He was already guessing that they would be the kinds of things that would make George seem like a great guy.

He couldn't quite pinpoint what his father was up to, but he was sure it was something.

"Well, for one thing," Grace said, "when he came over to talk to you that night after we'd done that art class...?"

John nodded briefly. He was glad that she hadn't thought it necessary to remind him that he hadn't stuck around for the conversation.

"He was leading a Bible study that night," Grace continued. "He also leads a men's prayer group at church before the service on Sunday mornings. I've heard such good things about it. I've also seen him doing volunteer work at the food bank. He's basically willing to give a helping hand to anyone who needs it."

John processed this glowing review, but instead of it reassuring him, tight twin knots of anger settled in his stomach and throat. He was honestly worried for the people that George was drawing in with whatever this new game of his was.

But could a person who was only playing a game really write those articles that represented such a deep understanding of the comfort and reassurance that people craved?

"John?" Grace's worried voice drew him out of his thoughts. "What is it with you and your father?"

"I'm not sure you want to hear the answer."

She hesitated for as long as it took for him to

breathe in, and by the time he let his breath out again, her warm hand was covering his.

"I do," she said. "I don't understand, but I want to."

The oddest but most wonderful thing happened. John was no longer thinking about his father. The knots dissolved as he studied Grace's face, the face that had grown so dear to him in this short period of time.

Not stopping to think, he leaned forward until their lips touched.

It was like coming home to everything he'd longed for—everything sweet and warm and loving. All the things he had longed for and didn't think he would ever have were bestowed on him by Grace's beautiful mouth.

Chapter Thirteen

Grace's eyes flew open in surprise, and she drew back. The expression in her eyes was a mix of shy pleasure and skepticism.

"I'm not going to let you distract me from the question," she joked in a nervous way, "but nice try."

The merry-go-round in John's heart ground to a halt.

"I crossed a line," he said. "I'm sorry."

"That's okay." Grace touched her lips with her fingertips in a way that gave John hope that he wasn't the only one who had enjoyed the kiss, as unexpected as it was.

"I'm just… I guess I'm a little confused," she said.

"Me too," John said without humor. To give himself time to return to the real reason for their meeting, he stood up and put the coffee supplies away.

He sensed Grace watching him. By the time he sat down again, he knew what he had to say.

"I'm sorry I kissed you only because it was presumptuous," he began. "But kissing you was one of the best things I've done in a long time."

Grace's cheeks went pink as her mouth tried to decide whether to smile or not. But then a tiny grin won out, and she confessed, "I'm not sorry either."

The words almost made him go in for another kiss.

"But I am sorry if it makes either of us think this could turn into a relationship, because that's just not what I'm looking for these days, and I don't think you are either."

He didn't tell her that her blend of practicality and vulnerability made him think that maybe he *was* looking for something.

"We were talking about your father," she reminded him, ever so subtly easing her chair back to increase the distance between them.

John folded his arms across his chest, as if he too wanted to protect himself from any idea that the kiss could mean more than a fleeting moment of pleasure.

"You asked what was wrong between my father and me." He could hear his voice growing distant, a bit expressionless.

She nodded.

"The answer to that is that there is so much wrong that I don't even know where to start."

As succinctly and with as little drama and coloration as he could manage, John laid out the sad facts of his childhood: The story of a boy whose father prioritized his addictions above all else, including his family. A boy whose mother had abandoned him, leaving him with this same father. A boy who had a little brother he remembered only in dreams or sometimes in Toby's face.

"I'm not telling you this to gain your sympathy. I left that boy behind as best I could a long time ago." John experienced a bone-deep weariness unlike anything he'd ever felt before. Yet there was a sense of relief. He couldn't control how Grace reacted to the things he'd told her, and he definitely couldn't control whether or not she believed him. He could only hope and pray that she took his words to heart and wouldn't let George deep enough into her life to hurt her.

Grace's thoughts did a wild dance as she tried to coordinate John's description of his father with the George Bishop she had come to like a great deal. She respected and admired George, but she could see John's eyes asking what he dared not ask out loud. *Do you believe me?*

The things he had shared with her were hard to get her head around, but she did believe him. Not only because she had learned through her support group how commitment to sobriety could truly change people at their very core, but also because she knew John wouldn't lie to her.

But could I lie to him?

Wasn't that what she was doing by not telling him the truth about her own alcohol addiction?

No, she reasoned with herself, there was no reason to reveal her secret. Anything between them—whatever it was—was only temporary.

The only reason she could or should care about John's painful past with his father was because she knew both from personal experience and from hearing others share their experiences how freeing it was to let go.

"Do you think there's any possibility you could forgive him?" Grace asked. She folded her napkin one last time into a compact square and set it to the side out of reach. "Whatever kind of person he was, I really believe he's changed."

"And I don't," John said bluntly. He stood up. "I can't tell you what to do, Grace. But I want you to know that I haven't ever shared that much with anyone, and the reason I did is because I care so much about you. I care about Toby too, and I want you to be careful."

"I'm not sure what to say." Grace stood up too. The conversation didn't feel anywhere close to being over, but she had her work to get back to.

"What I would like…" John began to speak, then stopped and shook his head.

"What would you like?" Grace urged him.

Why did she want him to say that he would like to be part of her life even after she'd already told him—and herself—that wasn't the best idea?

John stepped forward again and took her hands in his.

"I want to get to know you better. I want to continue to help Toby in whatever way I can. I want to repair the reputation of the newspaper. I want to feel at peace for once in my life…"

Grace looked up at him, at the emotions warring on his face.

"Can we please be…friends?" he asked softly. "Be whatever this is? Because I'm not ready to let it go. I can't force you to keep your distance from George, even though everything I told you is the absolute truth. But can we please just be… us, and not have him be part of it?"

Grace's thoughts were troubled. But John's reaction to the suggestion that he forgive his father told her that she had made the right choice to stay silent about her drinking. And with that secret between them, how close could they really get?

As John stood there, she could look past his height and brawn, past his rugged features and past his deceptively gruff expression. She could see the little boy he had been and the sweet, gentle man that he was.

"I want that too," she said before she could stop herself. "I want us to be...whatever we are."

She didn't know why his wide, relieved grin made her want to cry instead of smile back.

September had always been Grace's favorite month. To her, it always signaled new beginnings, and she always experienced a sweet sorrow when it gave way to October.

With valued input from Adventures in Learning and from Blanche Collins, Grace agreed that it wouldn't hurt Toby to wait another year before advancing to AIL's kindergarten classroom.

"He's making wonderful progress," Ruby Kaiswatum assured Grace. "But there's no reason to rush things. He hasn't had easy formative years, and these things take time."

Every time Grace heard something like that said about Toby, she couldn't help thinking about the little boy John had been.

She believed that his father had changed. She believed that people *were* capable of change. But she also knew that wasn't a belief she could force on anyone, especially not someone like John.

She gave the issue over to God. She knew that was the right thing to do. If she was being honest, it was also because she simply wanted to enjoy the pleasure of John's company without any obstacles between them.

October days sped by, and autumn revealed itself in glorious yellow-golds and rich browns that signaled change and whispered of hope.

Most evenings, John found a reason to be with her and Toby. Gradually, they stopped looking for reasons, or needing to look for them, and spending time together came as naturally as if they'd always done it.

It took every ounce of willpower that Grace had not to settle into the relationship that wasn't a relationship. Every day, especially since he had shared the full truth of his childhood, she couldn't help thinking about what she was keeping from him.

But she couldn't even imagine telling him either. Not when this wasn't permanent… But the knot in her stomach grew larger.

One night, after they'd said prayers, Grace was tucking Toby in and noticed he was gazing up at her. Since his face had filled out more, his eyes, though still big, didn't look nearly as large and out of place in his face.

"Grace?" he said sleepily.

"What is it, my boy?"

"Are you always going to be my mom?"

Her breath caught as she willed back her

tears. She didn't want Toby to think he had said or done anything wrong.

Of course, as a foster mother, she had been prepared—as well as anyone *could* be prepared—for questions like that one. The most heartbreaking one was when a child asked why their real parents couldn't take care of them.

Grace had prepared herself for that question, even though other than Toby's nighttime anguish, which he seemed to mostly be over, he never said much about his mother. He was comfortable enough around her now, but he was still distant, still saving most of his chatter and open affection for John. She hadn't considered that he might be starting to think of her as his mother.

She reached in deep, past the torrent of emotions that swirled within her, and she pulled out the answer she knew she was supposed to give.

"You have a mother, Toby," she said gently. "She is away trying to get better so that she can be a better mother to you. I know that she loves you very much." She prayed daily that was true. "I am your foster mother, which means I'll be here to take care of you as long as you need me, until your real mother can take care of you again. Do you understand?"

"Yup," Toby said drowsily. He snuggled over and put his head on Grace's shoulder. "I know you'll stay."

It was a good thing he had closed his eyes then, because she could no longer hold back the tears that came rushing out.

A week later, they were at community center activities where John was going to teach his first photography class. Grace was offering some vegetarian recipe options for the upcoming holiday season. Toby had been excited to go ahead with the Harts to get good seats for the family movie that was being shown.

"He asked you if you were always going to be his mom?" John asked. He looked at Grace in the seat across from him. They still had a few minutes before they had to go in, so they were taking time to talk about what Grace had shared with him on the way over.

Seeing the expression on her face was like being in the middle of a book and not being able to guess if it would have a sad or happy ending. "That must have been quite the emotional wallop."

Grace nodded. "It sure was, and he cuddled up next to me. He never does things like that."

"What did you tell him?" John resisted the urge to reach out and draw her in to cuddle with him.

"I told him the truth. I said that he had a mom and that I was his foster mother. That I would take care of him as long as he needed."

"But that time could be coming to an end sooner than you want it to." John affirmed her feelings. He had never seen strong, practical Grace look so vulnerable.

"Am I a bad person, John? I must be." She sighed softly, and her lower lip trembled a bit until she corrected it with a bite. "I should be happy that Tiffany is getting well, and I am… I am. I'm just going to miss Toby so much."

There had been a time on a photo shoot at a big-city zoo when John had gotten too close to the polar bears' habitat trying to get the perfect shot. The cuteness of polar bears in movies and on commercials was a myth. They were majestic. They were stunning. They were also among the most dangerous predators on earth.

Suddenly, one of the beautiful white beasts had charged toward the area where John was taking his pictures. He swore afterward that he could actually see the saliva collecting around those knife-sharp teeth. He had stumbled backward, knocking the wind out of himself and ruining one of his best cameras.

He realized that he hadn't felt nearly as helpless then as he did now. He didn't know how to make Grace feel better.

"You'll still be part of his life in some way, won't you?" he asked.

She nodded. "Open communication between

parents and foster parents is always encouraged. Tiffany and I— Well, it's been very difficult for her. She hasn't been capable of reaching out while she works through things, and I don't want to push her, and…" The words came out in a rush of honesty. "I enjoyed being able to pretend that Toby really is mine. I must sound like a terrible person."

"Grace." This time, John didn't resist his urge to reach out to her. He enveloped her hands in his. "Grace," he repeated. "You're about as far from being a terrible person as anyone could possibly get. You are a person who loves deeply and only wants the best for Toby. No one can fault you for that."

She smiled somewhat tremulously, but her eyes shone.

The car filled with a waiting kind of silence. Then she said, "We'd better go in."

For a moment, John could hardly remember where they were or what he was supposed to be doing.

Just before she opened her door, he said, "Please wait. We'll go in right away, but there's something I want to say first."

"Okay…" She nervously tucked her hair behind her ears.

Now that she was waiting for what he had to say, John prayed that the unnamable feeling he carried in his heart would somehow make it through his mouth in a coherent manner.

"I want to be…someone…to you, Grace. I know it's far too soon to be putting any kind of label on what we are, and honestly, I don't want to label it. But I want to be someone you know you can count on, someone who reminds you what a wonderful person you are and how much you have to offer."

"I… I think…" Grace stammered. "I think I might like that. But, John, you know I don't *need* it. My parents… Well, they never made a fuss over each other, over me or the things I've accomplished. I always believed it was just expected of me."

"Maybe it's about time someone did make a big deal out of you and the things you do," John insisted.

"I just don't want you to feel obligated," Grace said. "Or to feel sorry for me because of Toby."

John looked her deep in the eyes, and in a gesture so gentle and careful it was almost like it was in slow motion, he reached out his hand and pushed a strand of hair off her cheek.

"Obligated," he said with his voice almost a whisper, "is the last thing I feel, Grace."

Chapter Fourteen

Someone at the alcoholics' support group had once said, "You live your life a certain way for so long, and you can't even imagine it being any other way. There's not even a question of imagining anything else, because the possibility of a different kind of life isn't even on your radar. But then something changes, and suddenly, you can see life in a different way. After a while, you look back, and you can't imagine your old life."

Grace found herself thinking about those words many times over the next few weeks as her relationship with John continued to unfold.

It was true that in some ways, nothing had changed. She still had her job in a profession she was proud of, and she did her best at it each day. The schedule adjustments she'd made that accommodated Toby's needs only made her work harder during the time she was in the office. She still coordinated activities for the community center, and it seemed that those were getting more busy and diverse than ever.

But now those things existed alongside her relationship with John. Yes, she would say now that it was a relationship. She was still Grace Severight, but now the patterns of her life included a wonderful man. They didn't ask or expect to change one another, they compatibly existed in each other's worlds, and she couldn't get over how easy and natural it was.

It was a Saturday morning in October. They were in her kitchen, and John had just told her that he intended to stay in Living Skies for good.

Toby was out having his supervised visit with his mother today and Grace was grateful for John's company and for his announcement that distracted her from her worry over Toby.

"Why do you want to stay?" Grace asked, cautious hope lighting in her heart. Even though she knew that no one person should be another person's sole reason for doing something, she couldn't help wanting to hear that she was at least part of that reason.

She and John still hadn't named their relationship anything but a friendship, but she could easily imagine that the time they spent together meant more to him each day, as it did with her.

Even if he never said the words, the answer was in his willingness to listen, to be there when she needed him for whatever reason. He was there to encourage, to be a cheerleader or a coach, to be the best friend she'd ever had.

Each day, it brought an indescribable joy to try to be all of that for him. She had faced many challenges in her life, but none greater or more rewarding than learning how to count on someone besides herself.

John's forehead creased in his endearing frown. Grace appreciated the way he always took time to give consideration to the questions that were important to her, and she trusted that he would speak from his heart.

He sat across from her at her kitchen table, looming large in the chair. It was a sight that was still enticingly strange to Grace. Yet it was also somehow comforting and familiar, like he truly belonged here.

"I want to stay because of you," John said. "I'm not going to pretend otherwise. I wouldn't have believed that it could happen, but in a short time, I've opened up to you more than I ever have with anyone. I feel so...so at home with you, Grace. You give me that sense of home, that kind of security and comfort I didn't think I would ever find. You've even helped restore some of my faith just by the example you set."

The words enveloped Grace like a warm hug,

but she still knew she couldn't be his sole reason for staying.

"I love hearing that, John," she said. "I can't believe either how much I've grown to care for you. But I need to know that life here in Living Skies is really what you want."

"It is," John said, drawing the words out slowly. "I've realized that I can't keep running, and I don't want to." His gaze was like a warm embrace. "You taught me that. I also realize that I haven't done the work I need to do with George. If I'm being honest, I don't know if I ever will be willing to do that. But I am willing to keep learning how not to let it define me."

Grace nodded, listening carefully.

"I've also discovered that I like running the newspaper," John continued. "It's not just a problem to be patched together as quickly as I can manage. It's a place where I know I have a purpose, and I know I can help things to keep getting better there.

"And, of course, there's Toby. I never had the chance to be the kind of brother I wanted to be for Simon, but your generosity in letting me be part of Toby's life has shown me that I can still make a difference to kids like Toby and I'm so grateful for that."

At the mention of Toby, worry returned and made a fist in Grace's stomach.

As always, John read her face like a scene he was framing for a photograph.

"You're worried about Toby." It wasn't even a question.

"I am," Grace conceded.

She'd thought about putting up a confident front, but John already knew that she was worried, and hadn't the last several weeks been about learning that she didn't have to pretend? Not with someone like John, who made it clear every day that he accepted and admired her.

"That's part of what I'm trying to say here," John said. "You don't have to be alone in your worry. You don't have to be alone in any of it. Grace, I'm here for all the reasons that I told you. I won't deny that I'm here for you, just as I know you're here for me. I don't think there's anything we can't face together. I know I can count on you, and I want you to know that you can count on me."

It was clear from all John had said that he wanted there to be something between them. She wanted that too. She had always thought that she didn't want a relationship, or at least didn't believe that she was cut out for one. But the more she got to know John, the more she realized that with the right person, she didn't have to change who she was.

But there was still that one thing that he didn't

know about her. That one thing she was worried might change everything.

Or would it? Maybe it was time to trust completely.

Grace had to tell him. She knew with the relief of realizing she could shake off a heavy coat in unseasonable weather that she had to tell him. There was no possible way they could ever move forward and explore what could be between them if she held on to her secret any longer. It would be a constant barrier between them that would keep her from giving her whole self to the relationship.

She glanced at the time. Toby would be home soon, and if she didn't speak now, she didn't know if she would ever get up the nerve again. She knew she couldn't stand to wait any longer.

"I want you to stay, John," she said. "I want that more than anything, and I want us to keep getting to know one another, because I think there is something really, really great here, and I think you know me well enough to know that I don't say that lightly."

John's face lit up with a wide smile but began to dim slightly when Grace added, "But there's something very important that you need to know about me, because if you don't know it, well, nothing we've said to each other will matter."

"Okay…" John's hand tightened around his

coffee mug, and he went still as he listened with his entire being.

Because she had never even imagined coming to such a moment, Grace realized that she had no words prepared. His apprehension quickly told her that the only kind thing to do was not drag it out and just say it.

"John… I'm an alcoholic."

His shoulders jerked involuntarily, and he gave one of those puzzled half laughs like he didn't get the punch line of a convoluted joke. "You're a what?"

Grace could see his eyes start to beg her to tell him that it was a joke. A cruel, tasteless, pointless and inappropriate joke, but a joke nonetheless.

"An alcoholic," she rasped out.

Still he gaped at her like she was speaking a language he'd never heard before.

She rushed into the opportunity that his silence gave her to explain. She hadn't had an alcoholic beverage in a long time. She regularly attended meetings. She was a good foster mother to Toby, a good friend to others, a good friend and possibly more to him. Everything he believed about her was still true.

"I'm still me," she finished.

Something worse than anger showed on his face, worse than sadness. It was the face of a stranger. Cold, withdrawn and, worst of all, the face of someone who wished that they remain strangers.

"What you are," John said in a voice chillingly remote and almost casual, "is a liar. Of course, that goes with the territory."

"I'm not," Grace tried to protest. "It's just not something I have reason to tell people most of the time. It doesn't impact my daily life anymore. I didn't tell you because…because I didn't think you'd become nearly as important to me as you have."

"And those times that we talked about my father," John continued, like her words had bounced right off of him, "how he treated me, how he hurt me… You didn't think it was fair to give me a warning then? You knew I couldn't possibly love someone who was anything like him. Are you that selfish, Grace? I trusted you with my pain. Didn't that mean anything to you?"

For a moment, his voice faltered, then he pulled himself together with angry determination.

"John, if you would just—"

"If I would just what, Grace?" His voice was a whip. He stood up. "There's nothing you can say now to make a difference. There's nothing I want to hear from you ever again."

Grace couldn't move from her seat as he showed himself out. She waited to hear the door slam, but John closed it slowly and carefully behind him. Somehow, that was worse.

The next day, when Blanche reported that the visit had gone well and that the paperwork was in motion to return Toby to his mother, Grace was still so numb that the news hardly registered.

She dully reminded herself that she had always thought she was meant to be alone.

Two weeks after Grace's devastating confession, John locked the door of *The Chronicle*'s office and slipped the key into the pocket of his blue jeans. He would make time soon to give the key back to Vivian.

He knew she was disappointed about his decision to leave the paper again, but he hoped that she would eventually come to understand that this decision was the best one under the circumstances. He took some comfort in knowing that he had repaired the newspaper's reputation, and the citizens of Living Skies once again knew they could trust what was written there.

But he couldn't stay. He had done his best to quell the inner warnings that there were reasons why he never let himself get too close to anyone. Going forward, he vowed that he would always remember those warnings were given to him for a reason.

As he started his walk back to the apartment he was renting, his hands jammed into his pockets of his jacket, his shoulders hunched against the chill autumn evening, there was something else that persisted beneath the wall he was determined to rebuild. Something that wanted to slide the bricks out to topple it.

He turned the corner and saw his father at the corner waiting to cross the street.

John froze.

Then, for reasons he would never be able to explain, he remembered some Bible passages he had read about the vicious, Christian-persecuting Saul's transformation into Christianity's greatest advocate, Paul.

And, like Paul, what had been blinding him fell away.

When John looked at his father, he didn't see a saint, but he didn't see a monster either. He simply saw a man who was trying to get by in this complicated, ever-changing life in the best way he could.

As John watched his father cross the street, he thought that maybe forgiveness meant being willing to acknowledge another person's humanness. To acknowledge that everyone—including his father and including Grace—was simply doing their best.

Dear God, what am I doing? What have I done?

He had to see Grace and apologize. He had to acknowledge his deep error in judging her. Even if she never wanted to have anything to do with him again, he needed to say the words to her as much as he needed to take his next breath.

He loved her and didn't want to live his life without her.

But he didn't know what to say, where to begin. His prayers became a knot of confusion and guilt, impossible to untangle. Then, like a light shining through the darkness, he knew who would know.

His father.

Chapter Fifteen

On Friday evening, John stood on the steps of the house where his father now lived.

Darkness was setting in by suppertime, so the streetlights were on. There was a chill in the air, but that wasn't the only reason John trembled inside his brown-plaid jacket.

He could see that the yard was neatly kept, and the house was a modest size. It too looked like George had developed some homeowner's pride.

I sure hope You're with me, Lord, because I would not have come up with this idea on my own.

Taking a deep breath, he reached out and knocked on the front door, waited a moment and then rang the doorbell. He shifted from one foot to the other, half hoping that his father wasn't home and he'd have an excuse to turn and leave.

No, this was about Grace. He had a reason

for being here, even if it wasn't to mend fences with his father quite yet.

The door began to open, and John could already feel his jaw pushing forward aggressively.

But then George said, "John?" in an almost awestruck way, and he felt some of the tension flowing out of him.

"Can I come in?" he asked.

George blinked. "Of course, son. Of course you can." He stepped back and made a gesture of welcome. "I'm so happy to see you. I don't mind telling you that I've prayed for this day, but I didn't honestly think it would ever come."

"I'm not here about you and me," John said. He knew he was being on the rude side, but he couldn't let George think that he was there for some serious father-son bonding time.

George wrinkled his forehead in the concentrating frown that John had felt many times on his own face.

"May I ask why you are here?" he said. "Whatever the reason is, John, I *am* so glad to see you. Would you like to take off your coat? Are you hungry? Would you like something to drink?"

John shrugged off his coat, which George took from him and hung inside the front closet, but he declined the other two offers.

"Come in," George repeated. "Please sit down."

John sat on the edge of a brown couch and took in the room with his practiced eye. It was small, clean and clearly the home where a man of faith lived. The artwork was sparse but paid tribute to that fact, as did the obviously well-used Bible that lay open on the coffee table.

George sat in an armchair opposite the couch and waited for John to begin talking.

As John absorbed his father's expectant but patient face, it occurred to him that the only agitation in the room came from him. George was calm, if a bit puzzled by his son's visit and the reason for it. One might even say that it was peaceful being in his presence.

"So, you read this?" John blurted out, gesturing at the open Bible.

If George was surprised at the non sequitur, he didn't show it.

"Wouldn't go a day without," he said. "Do you have a Bible?"

"No... I've been thinking about getting one though."

George stood up and walked to a bookcase. "I have several. I could give you one." He pulled a couple off of the shelf. "Do you have any idea what translation you prefer?"

John shook his head. This was all too strange, making polite chitchat about Bibles. He retreated into bluntness again. "I don't want one of your Bibles."

George hesitated, nodded and put the Bibles back.

Help me, Lord, John prayed. He knew he either had to say what he'd come for—if he even fully knew himself—or leave.

"You know Grace Severight?" he asked.

George nodded. "I do. She's a lovely woman. I've heard you're close."

So, his father kept tabs on him, or at the very least was party to the small-town grapevine.

"I thought we were," John said, doing his best to squash any emotion out of his voice. "But I recently found something out about her that changes everything."

George returned to his chair and looked at John with kind, sad eyes. "Out of respect for Grace, I won't say, but I suspect I know what you found out."

"She says she's changed," John continued. "I want to believe her."

He looked his father full in the face. "She says that you've changed, but..."

"But you have a hard time believing that," George finished for him. "And if you can't believe I've changed, why should you believe that Grace won't disappoint you again. Am I right?"

John hesitated and then nodded.

"Well, John," George said, "I can't give you any guarantees about myself, and I certainly can't about another person. Now, I know that's likely not what you want to hear, but it's the truth of it. We could try to prove ourselves to you from now to the Second Coming, but none of us have any control over what you decide about us."

"So, what am I supposed to do?" John asked.

"Ah, son," George said, and John could hear a world of love, regret and hard-earned wisdom in those two syllables. "I can't tell you what you're supposed to do. But I can tell you that you have the power to decide. It's within your control. You can hold grudges, or you can let go. You can forgive or not. I can tell you one thing though. Holding on is a lot more exhausting than letting go. Think about it."

John gave one terse nod.

"Can I pray with you?" George asked.

John's first instinct was to say no, but then something nudged his heart, asking him if he wasn't getting tired of carrying this burden.

Saying yes could be a step to letting go. A step that he knew he needed to take.

"Dear Lord," George prayed. "Thank You for bringing my son here tonight. I know I have made more mistakes in the past than I can count and there's nothing I can do to change that. But I also know that You are a God who forgives profoundly. I'm asking You to please open John's heart to the possibility of a restored relationship and to keep my own heart open and humble as I continue moving forward. I ask all this in Jesus's name. Amen."

"Amen," John echoed.

He opened his eyes and his father was looking at him, smiling softly.

John met his gaze, and although he wasn't quite ready to smile back, he didn't look away.

After a series of supervised and then a few unsupervised visits with intensive follow-up, the decision was made that Toby would be returned to the full custody of his mother.

"Bring this up in conversation with him whenever there's an opportunity," Blanche Collins had coached Grace. "We don't want him feeling blindsided. Remind him every day how many days he has left with you. Be open to his questions…"

Without doubt, the hardest advice of all to follow was, "Don't let your own emotions get in the way. We wouldn't be allowing Tiffany to have custody of Toby again if we didn't believe she was ready in every way to care for him, but it's still going to be a huge adjustment for Toby.

You can greatly help the process by showing him that you're okay with it."

But Grace wasn't okay, not that there was much these days she was okay with.

The days marched relentlessly by and on a November morning that whispered of the winter to come, even while multicolored leaves still adorned the ground, Grace closed the suitcase filled with Toby's belongings and prayed for the strength to say goodbye without breaking down.

She sat on his bed and Toby stood in front of her fidgeting, sticking his fingers in his mouth.

"I have something for you," Grace said. She reached behind her and produced the book she had tucked out of sight. It was Toby's favorite library book, the one with the photographs of animals and nature.

The one that had connected them to John...

"This one is yours to keep," Grace said, putting it in his hands. "It doesn't need to go back to the library."

Toby studied it but didn't say anything.

"You'll have your camera too," Grace said. "You can keep taking pictures of things."

"Does my mom know about taking pictures?" Toby asked.

"I'm sure she'd love to hear about it."

"What if…" Toby whispered as he looked at his feet. Then he looked up and the question came out in a rush. "What if she doesn't like me again?"

In that moment, Grace realized how much Toby's loyalty to his mother had been a conscious decision he made each day. It wasn't something that came easily or naturally at all. What an enormous decision for such a small boy to have to make.

"She will love you, Toby," Grace said, choking back an emotional torrent. She reached out and stroked his arm. "She *does* love you and she always has. Sometimes people need help being the best people they can be. Your mom took time to get that help so she could take the very best care of you."

Toby considered this, hugging the book to his chest.

Grace checked the time on her phone and stood up.

"Ms. Collins will be here soon," she said. "Come on, bring your book and your camera, I'll carry your suitcase."

"Grace?"

"Yes, Toby?"

He flung himself at her and threw his arms around her. "I'm gonna miss you," he said.

Grace hugged him back, finally letting her tears flow.

"I'm going to miss you too, Toby. But I'll always be here for you."

* * *

"Thanks for coming for lunch, Jenny," Grace said on the following Saturday afternoon. "I guess I'm still getting used to how empty the house feels without Toby here."

"David took the girls to run errands. I was happy to come," Jenny said. She stepped inside, hung her coat up and gave Grace a quick hug. "You know you can call anytime or pop over, right?"

Grace nodded. "I appreciate that," she said. "Come in. Lunch is ready."

They sat at Grace's kitchen table with bowls of chicken noodle soup cooling in front of them.

"Not a very adult meal." Grace gestured to the bowl. "I guess I'm still used to making a five-year-old's favorite."

"It smells delicious," Jenny assured her. "I don't think there's an age limit on enjoying chicken noodle soup. Should I pray?"

Grace had already picked her spoon up and set it down softly.

"If you want to."

Instead of saying the blessing, Jenny asked, "Are you okay, Grace? It's not just Toby, is it?"

Grace shrugged. The attempt at a casual gesture was next to impossible to pull off while deep loneliness devoured her insides like a wolf swallowing up a lamb.

"It doesn't matter," she managed to get out. She pictured the words hopping out of her mouth like frogs and toads in the old fairy tale. "I got along without... Toby before, and I'll get along without him now."

"And John?" Jenny prompted gently.

Grace shook her head vigorously. "Some things just aren't meant to be."

"You don't really believe that, do you?"

Grace met her friend's concerned eyes. "I've always done okay on my own."

"No one doubts that, Grace. I've always admired you for your strength and independence, but I also wonder..."

"What?" Grace asked, pretty sure that she already knew the answer. She was unsure if she would be able to answer honestly if it was the question she dreaded.

"Are you independent because that is truly your choice or because you're afraid that if you let anyone get to know you, you might get hurt?"

"Might get hurt?" Grace's voice scraped over what felt like broken glass in her throat. "I was hurt. I *am* hurt."

"Ah, so you admit it," Jenny said very softly. "So, what happens now?"

"I have no idea." Grace took a spoonful of soup and raised it to her mouth, but then her shoulders slouched, and she returned the soup to the bowl.

"Maybe the first step is admitting that you can't go backward," Jenny said.

"What do you mean?"

Jenny set her own soupspoon down.

"Grace, as long as I've known you, you've had this way about you. You're smart, you're successful and you're strong. But you've always had this wall up that keeps people out. I don't know if it's just your personality or the way you were raised or…or your addiction that you keep hidden like it's something to be ashamed of when you really should be so proud of yourself for overcoming it."

Grace was silent, listening.

"But at least you know now that you can let that wall down," Jenny continued. "You can take a risk, and I promise that someday you're going to find out that it's worth doing."

Grace tried to imagine letting her guard down again—letting it down for someone besides John—and she simply couldn't.

"I know I'm doing a bad job of convincing you," Jenny said, "so I'm just going to be quiet now and eat this soup, which, by the way, smells delicious. But think about what I've said. Please?"

Grace nodded simply to get the conversation

over with and began to eat her own soup, though she had no appetite for it.

Jenny was three mouthfuls in when she stopped, swallowed and said, "I completely forgot to give thanks."

"I think God will let it slide," Grace said.

"Speaking of that…" Jenny paused. "Okay, I know I said I wasn't going to raise the topic again, but I have to tell you that yesterday I saw John and George praying over their meals at Murphy's."

"Yesterday?" Grace repeated. She swallowed. "John is still in town?"

"Looks that way," Jenny said. "I have to say they looked like they were involved in a pretty deep conversation about something."

"I didn't know…" Grace said almost to herself. "I didn't know he stayed. I didn't think he would ever forgive his father enough to have a meal and a conversation with him."

"But he did," Jenny said with an almost triumphant gleam in her eye. "And I think if you asked him why, he would say it was because of you."

After Jenny left, Grace mused over their conversation as she cleaned the kitchen. Once everything was clean and back in its place, she tried to engage in some Bible reading. Sipping on her midafternoon cup of chamomile mint tea as she gazed out the window, she let God's autumn paintbrush soothe her soul.

He didn't leave. He's talking to his father. He didn't leave...

She was too weary to sort it all out. She suddenly had the comfortable, drowsy feeling of being a child in the back seat of a car during a long trip, trusting that someone bigger than her would take care of things.

The one thing she did know was that Jenny was right about one thing. There was no going backward. Opening her heart and being honest about herself would mean she risked hurt and rejection. But not doing it would mean she would never be as fully herself as God wanted her to be. Jesus had not died for half a person. He had died for every single part of her.

Grace was taking her cup into the kitchen when the doorbell rang. A bit startled and more than a bit puzzled, she went to open the door.

John stood on the doorstep.

"Don't slam the door in my face," he said.

"I wasn't going to." Her heart began a slow, faltering dance to a tune she didn't yet dare believe she could hear.

"I came to tell you that I was wrong." John's hands twisted together so tightly she could feel the pain in her own. "I was wrong to judge you.

I was wrong to leave. And I'm sorrier than you'll ever know."

Grace let the words wash over her. They were a start, but she knew now that she needed more.

"Are you... Would you like to come in?"

John stepped into her home.

"Are you staying?" She got the question out.

"I can for a little while," John said, a cautiously hopeful light creeping into his eyes. "I said I would meet David and some of the guys for coffee, but if I'm not putting you out, I can stay."

"No." Grace swallowed. The taste in her throat wasn't quite as bitter as it had been earlier. "I mean, are you staying in Living Skies?"

"I think that's up to you."

She shook her head. "No, it isn't. You need to have your own reasons to stay."

John frowned, a look that she had long ago learned made him appear fierce but really meant that he was thinking deeply, that he cared.

Funny how his frown had become one of the most endearing things about him.

"If you mean getting to know my father better and running a newspaper, then yes, I have reasons to stay. But there is only one reason I *want* to stay. Grace, I love you."

They were three simple words. Simple words, but the hardest, most complicated and most profound to say if a man and a woman meant those words the way God intended.

If she said them, Grace knew it would mean a forever thing. It would mean trusting John to see her and to love her at her most vulnerable and worst moments, as well as at her best. It would mean not only forgiving him for his error but forgiving the many that would follow—just as he would need to forgive hers, because they were both only human. It would mean being at each other's side no matter what life brought their way.

But not saying them would mean betraying herself at the deepest core of who she knew she wanted to be. She loved John Bishop, and to say anything else would be a lie.

"I love you too," she said.

"I want to spend my life with you."

"I want that too."

John lifted her up, twirled her around and set her down again. Then he kissed her for a blissful amount of time, long enough to send doubts scurrying away.

"I'll get you the prettiest ring you've ever seen," John promised. "And I'll propose in the proper way, down on one knee and everything."

"Whenever and however you do it," Grace said, her heart singing, "it will be just right, because it will be what's right for us."

"I just have one concern," John said.

"What's that?" Grace could feel her forehead creasing.

"Since I expect to be busy at our wedding, being the groom and all, I don't know who's going to take the pictures."

"I think we can work it out," Grace said, laughing. "Now, please kiss me again."

John did, and she gave thanks to God for this man who knew her completely and would love her well.

Epilogue

How did it get to be the end of November already? Grace wondered on a Sunday afternoon as she and Tiffany Bower sprinkled red and green sprinkles on the sugar cookies that Toby was going to take to his kindergarten class the next day.

John and Toby were taking photographs of the undecorated tree from all angles. They planned to take pictures through all stages of decorating so that John could teach Toby about something called a photo series.

A mere five months ago, Grace had been a June bride, one *The Chronicle*—with perhaps just a bit of bias—had called the most beautiful bride ever. Grace didn't know about that, but she was sure she was the happiest one.

She hadn't known or admitted that she wanted a husband, but she truly couldn't imagine her life without John now. She continued to see God's hand in other areas of their life too.

John and George met for a weekly coffee, often using the time to chat about Scriptures. While they both agreed that they couldn't change the past and George couldn't suddenly be the father that John had learned to live without, they were both making the effort to make a connection based on the men they were today.

Toby continued to blossom and thrive in kindergarten under the guidance of the wonderful staff at Adventures in Learning. His mother, Tiffany, had stayed clean and was on the path of healing emotionally. She was facing her depression with courage and determination, and in doing so, she was daily gaining the confidence that she needed to be a good mother.

Any pain that Grace had experienced in having to surrender Toby back to his birth mother was soothed by the healing balm of seeing their obvious love for one another.

Most of all, there was John, her gentle bear of a husband. He continued to teach her—sometimes unknowingly—to pay attention to the small details and to see beauty in unexpected places. He reminded her daily that she was worthy of love and that being honest about needing someone was a sign of strength, not weakness.

Her loving husband had so much to bring to anyone's life.

That was why she couldn't wait any longer

to share news of an earlier phone call she'd had from Blanche Collins about a child who was up for adoption.

"Her name is Gloria," Grace told him as they curled up on the couch together after Tiffany and Toby had gone home. "She's ten years old and is a child with Down syndrome. Blanche says she has so much love to give."

John put his arm around her and gathered her in.

"So do we."

Nestled in the secure arms of her husband, Grace drank in their surroundings, which spoke of the season of joy and giving, and she treasured all God had already given them.

* * * * *

Dear Reader,

Thank you so much for reading this book. I hope that you enjoyed sharing in the journey of Grace and John.

We all have secrets. Sometimes they are good secrets, like planning a surprise party for someone or finding that perfect gift you can't wait to give a loved one.

Other times, though, keeping secrets can be harmful to us and to others. We may keep something secret because we are afraid no one will understand and we don't want to be judged.

Grace is keeping her alcoholism a secret and John is clinging to grudges from his past. But when they decide to open up and share their truths, they find their lives can move forward in a positive way.

Our Father God knows everything about us and He loves us profoundly. I pray that you remember that.

I truly believe that Love Inspired is blessed with the best readers ever and I'd love to hear from you. Please reach out to me at deelynn1000@hotmail. com, follow me on Twitter @dlgwritesl or Instagram @dlgwrites, or check out my new Facebook page, Donna Gartshore's Author Updates.

God Bless,
Donna